SARA DOUGLASS grew up in South Australia. After working as a nurse, she completed three degrees at the University of Adelaide, including a PhD in early modern English history. She worked as a Senior Lecturer in Medieval History at La Trobe University, Bendigo. After becoming a full-time writer, Sara moved to Tasmania, where she discovered a passion for gardening when she wasn't writing. The author of 20 novels, *The Hall of Lost Footsteps* is her only story collection.

SARA DOUGLASS died on 27 September 2011, aged 54, following a three-year struggle with cancer.

THE HALL OF
LOST FOOTSTEPS

Also by SARA DOUGLASS

The Axis Trilogy
   Battleaxe (1995)
   Enchanter (1996)
   StarMan (1996)
The Wayfarer Redemption
   Sinner (1997)
   Pilgrim (1998)
   Crusader (1999)
The Crucible
   The Nameless Day (2000)
   The Wounded Hawk (2001)
   The Crippled Angel (2002)
The Troy Game
   Hades' Daughter (2002)
   God's Concubine (2004)
   Darkwitch Rising (2005)
   Druid's Sword (2006)
Darkglass Mountain
   The Serpent Bride (2007)
   The Twisted Citadel (2008)
   The Infinity Gate (2010)

Beyond the Hanging Wall (1996)
Threshold (1997)
The Devil's Diadem (2011)

NON-FICTION

The Betrayal of Arthur (1998)

THE HALL OF LOST FOOTSTEPS

STORIES BY
SARA DOUGLASS

T℥
ᵽ℥ Ticonderoga
publications

to my readers
with thanks and love

The Hall of Lost Footsteps by Sara Douglass

Published by Ticonderoga Publications

Copyright © 2011 Sara Douglass Enterprises

Introduction copyright © 2011 Karen Brooks

"The Silence of the Dying" copyright © 2010 Sara Douglass Enterprises

Designed and edited by Russell B. Farr
Typeset in Sabon and Trajan Pro

A Cataloging-in-Publications entry for this title is available from the National Library of Australia.

ISBN 978-1-921857-02-7 (limited edition hardcover)
      978-1-921857-05-8 (hardcover)
      978-1-921857-06-5 (trade paperback)

Ticonderoga Publications
PO Box 29 Greenwood
Western Australia 6924

www.ticonderogapublications.com

10 9 8 7 6 5 4 3 2 1

I would like to thank Jeremy G Byrne, Jonathan Strahan, Richard Scriven, Jack Dann, Janeen Webb, Ramsey Campbell, Dennis Etchison, Ellen Datlow, Terri Windling, Deborah Thomas, Angela Slatter, Simon Brown, Kate Forsyth, Juliet Marillier, Kim Wilkins, Sean Williams, Russell B Farr, and Karen Brooks.

CONTENTS

INTRODUCTION

KAREN BROOKS

I first met Sara Douglass back in Bendigo, Victoria in 1992. Known then only as Dr Sara Warneke, I still remember the day a young, pretty blonde woman with intense blue-eyes, a wicked sense of humour and passion for medieval history, entered the lecture theatre at the Bendigo campus of La Trobe University.

Little did I know that day as she told an enraptured bunch of students about wars, kings, queens, pilgrims and saints that not only would she become one of my dearest friends, my soul-sister, as we like to say, but that in the not too-distant future she would emerge as one of Australia's most eminent writers of fantasy fiction as well.

Author of twenty-one books and many short stories, the latter that for the very first time are gathered in this marvellous volume, *The Hall of Lost Footsteps*, Sara's output has been prolific and constant. Known for her sweeping sagas that draw from different eras in world history as well as totally fabricated lands and peoples, she's attracted praise, awards, critical attention and a worldwide, very loyal fan-base.

While Sara's biographical details are merely a Google search away, what many people don't know about her is that she's an intensely private, loving, kind, funny, spiritual and pragmatic person.

Born in Penola, South Australia, the youngest of four children (she has two older sisters and a brother), Sara moved to Adelaide when she was seven. Losing her mother, Elinor, to ovarian cancer when she was just twelve years-old had a profound and lasting impact on Sara. Encouraged into nursing by her father, Bob and step-mum, Joan, she endured for seventeen long years. She began to plot her escape from a career she didn't like with a Bachelor of Arts at the University of Adelaide (majoring in politics!) before moving onto Honours and a PhD in 16th century English history.

Making her mark as a postgraduate student, Sara was called *stupor mundi*—the "wonder of the world"—by staff. Not only did she complete her dissertation before her scholarship expired, but she did it while nursing three days a week. In order to fill in time, she also edited a 17th century diary and, discovering the collection of British material at the Barr-Smith library of the university to be poorly catalogued, she created her own. It was so valuable to the history department that they purchased a copy.

An appointment as a lecturer in medieval history at the Bendigo campus of La Trobe University soon followed. Academic life, however, was not what Sara hoped. Gone were the days of immersion in research and dedicated students to be replaced by internecine wars between departments and faculty staff, long hours, little time to research and publish and, worse, a barely disguised misogyny that saw the young and talented Dr Warneke singled out for differential treatment.

Desperate to leave an occupation that demanded so much and gave so little in return, Sara's imagination, like the Icarii of her novels, took flight and the rest is genre history. Spending every spare minute on the keyboard hammering out a variety of tales was the way Sara escaped her demanding job and a means of ignoring the house she rented which, frankly, was a leaky, cold, mouldy horror.

Rejected for some early romance novels that, as one publisher described, while very well written had "too much plot", it wasn't long before Sara changed direction. Applying her vast knowledge of English history, she added doses of the supernatural, magic, non-human races and lashings of religion and conflict and *voila!* a trilogy was born.

Sending the manuscript to a literary agent she found in the phonebook (as it turns out, the discerning Lyn Tranter), the book was passed to one of Lyn's children to read and given the thumbs up. So, Sara secured an agent, a pseudonym, and a publishing deal followed.

The first book of what became known as The Axis Trilogy, *Battleaxe* was published to great success in 1995. The sequels, *Enchanter* and *Starman*, followed the year after. Attracting both critical and popular acclaim, these books not only gave Sara the financial freedom to buy and restore her beautiful house, Ashcotte, in Bendigo but to gradually leave academia and become a full-time writer. In the midst of writing her numerous books and these short stories, Sara moved to Cornelian Bay, Tasmania, and restored another lovely old house that she named Nonsuch. With soaring turrets and huge rooms filled with books and exquisite curios, it also has magnificent productive gardens over which Sara lovingly laboured, discovering a real passion for gardening and preserving. Sharing her home with five cuddly cats: Luther, Lady Jane Grey (Janey), Claude, Jack, and Cromwell, she also maintained two websites—one about her writing and books, the other about gardening. Over the years, Sara developed and encouraged a close-knit and supportive virtual community of writers, readers, gardeners and cat lovers, and once she joined FaceBook opened up to a new world of cyber friends and fans.

Having known Sara for almost twenty years, she also inspired me into a similar career path: first as an academic and then, later, as an author. Tired of hearing me say creative writing was something I wanted to do, in her usual forthright way Sara said to me, "stop saying you're going to do it and just do it." Great advice for any area of life: the notion that you shouldn't just talk about doing something, but find the courage to act, to try. That's the way Sara lives—and with no regrets.

I know I'm not the only writer who has benefitted from her patience, belief, straight-talking and inspiration. In fact, I don't think it's too far a stretch to argue that Sara, as a writer and a person, (re)opened the fantasy fiction door in Australia and, beckoning enthusiastically, invited other authors of speculative fiction to follow. Certainly, her success made it easier for a new crop of fantasy writers to be recognised and for their novels to be published and received, something her many awards and accolades haven't yet formally acknowledged.

As someone who's travelled most of the writing and personal journey with her, it hasn't been easy for Sara. What I mean by that is she works hard and realistically, treating writing as a business, as something to be taken seriously and not merely as an artistic endeavour, though that aspect is appreciated as well. This attitude is something she readily passes on through advice and role-modelling.

At the height of Sara's career, she was struck the cruellest of blows.

In late 2008, Sara was diagnosed with ovarian cancer. Since then, she's endured surgery, many rounds of chemotherapy and countless other medical interventions. At one stage, she wrote what to some people was a controversial blog entitled "The Silence of the Dying." To me, it was yet another example of the way in which Sara reaches out to those in need, gives a voice to those who lack one and refuses to accept platitudes and the comfortable option—in this case, of remaining quiet in the face of fear, uncertainty and anger. Expressing what it feels like to be given a terminal diagnosis, and the emotional, psychological and physical consequences of that is not an easy read, nor is it meant to be.

It's particularly relevant as I write this for, after an initial period of dormancy, Sara's cancer has, as we knew it would, returned. With her mantra "to do it" ringing in my ears, I moved to Tasmania to care for her along with my husband, Stephen. It was an easy decision for us to make. These last months with Sara have been bittersweet, filled with laughter, tears, pain, fear, and incredible closeness but above all, so much love.

It's no surprise then that love, lost, found, abused, neglected, passionate and unrequited, is one of the many themes in not only Sara's books, but also the short stories in this superb collection. Other tropes that recur throughout are birth, death, illness, relics, saints, superstition, magic, revenge, honour, the role of religion and faith in everyday life and fallen and falling women. These are the stuff upon which Douglass stories and dreams, and those of her readers, are made.

More than simply a gathering of Sara's short stories into one compilation, *The Hall of Lost Footsteps* is quite unique. Not only are there original tales drawn from history and often the periods in which her books are set, but there's also a section dedicated to The Axis Trilogy where some of the creative background and complex world-building that underpins not only the six books of The Wayfarer Redemption, but also the DarkGlass Mountain trilogy are realised. Stories such as "Fire Night", "The Rise of the Seneschal". "The Wars of the Axe", "How Axis Found His Axe", "How the Icarii Found Their Wings" and "The Coroleans" provide us with exceptional insights into the foundations and broader fictive landscape that Sara crafted in order to give her novels such depth, richness and verisimilitude. It's not often that we're given such a special peep into what makes a writer tick and it's yet again a credit to Sara that she shares this with us.

Beyond the central tales of Tencendor featured in this edition, is an imaginative feast of wonders. Set in the historical periods that Sara knows, loves and cherishes, are a range of diverse fables. From the opening story to the final one, there's a sense in which we step back into epochs and places both possible and impossible, where chivalry, honour, compassion and vengeance were codes by which people lived and where faith manifested in physical and spiritual realms, both of which, when the time and person was right, could be accessed.

As the title of her favourite novel, *Threshold*, and these stories suggest, it's the in-between spaces that continue to fascinate Sara—those borderlands that blur right and wrong, the secular and the immaterial, love and hate, truth and lies, respect and disrespect, the living and the dead. Most of the yarns within these pages reflect that attraction: "Of Fingers and Foreskins", is a story about a joust and the relics the two knights believe will preserve them and the woman who knows better; "The Mistress of Marwood Hagg", is a parable about death, birth and revenge; "Blackheart", "St Uncumber" and "The Evil Within", all explore the thin veils that separate the "real" world from the imagined one. They're also stories that display, within the context of the medieval worldview, the power of the feminine.

The strength of the writing is such that you're drawn inside a bedroom, church, work space, newly built train station, or graveyard and hover over the action, incapable of preventing the inevitable, privy to a triumph or tragedy or an admixture of both. As we read, we also bear witness to the movement on the page, the interior design of the character, yet unlike so many of Sara's protagonists, we live to tell the tale.

For if there's one thing Sara has never been afraid of when it comes to her characters, it's the gruesome (and often deserved) death. In fact, Sara and I would regularly and nervously joke about our characters meeting one day and plotting to pay us back for the lives and deaths we, as writers, have thrust upon them.

Despite the sometimes grisly ends a Douglass character meets, there's an over-riding sense of justice and of setting wrongs right that permeates her works—long and short—especially when these blunders arise from simple misunderstandings. In *The Hall of Lost Footsteps*, there are two very similar examples of this. "The Field of Thorns" is analogous to the story from which the book's title is taken and the last in the collection, "The Hall of Lost Footsteps". The premise of these tales is close: both feature heart-rending deaths, subsequent hauntings and the spiritual desolation these evoke, and which needs the understanding and gifts of a special person to put right.

Where they deviate is in effect and solution. At first glance, it may seem strange to include two such comparable stories in the one spine. But, by incorporating both, we're given an awareness of how a writer develops the kernel of an idea and how, with a tweak here, and a change of sex and motivation there, a different story with alternate emphasis can emerge. As a writer and reader, it's a treat to see first hand how another author's mind operates and I believe including both these stories is a boon for writers and fans of Sara alike.

Overall, *The Hall of Lost Footsteps* is a remarkable addition to the canon of Sara Douglass. Scary, witty, imbued with history and a sense of other-worldliness, evocative and full, these tales function as a magnificent companion to her novels and non-fiction work, the erudite, *The Betrayal of Arthur*.

When I was first asked to write this introduction, by Sara and her publisher, Russell B Farr, I was delighted, humbled and worried: concerned I couldn't do someone who's not only one of my closest friends and a writer of prodigious talent justice, but who has also been my inspiration, mentor and confidant for years. I still don't believe I have, but this is the only public chance I will get. We both expressed our excitement that, after all these years, we finally get our names on the same book. Truth is, I am piggybacking and Sara is generously carrying me. She would argue to the contrary, but for the first time in our friendship, she would be wrong.

As I draw this introduction to Sara's last stories to a close, it's with a heavy heart and a mind aching with unbelievable sorrow. Sara is in palliative care as I write, tired beyond all reason, sick to the core and preparing for that final sleep from which none us awake: at least, not into this world.

Wherever Sara journeys next, I know it will be on the wings of gentle fancy, in places beyond reasoning and care and where her bright, shining spirit will continue to soar. I know she will live on in the memories of those who were fortunate enough to know and love her and be loved in return, and that with her fantastical stories she'll continue to touch the lives and reveries of generations to come.

I now invite you to enter *The Hall of Lost Footsteps* and, if you dare, tread boldly and well and you will find a place of pure escapism and astonishing imagination.

You will find Sara Douglass.

KAREN BROOKS
HOBART, SEPTEMBER 2011

THE HALL OF LOST FOOTSTEPS

OF FINGERS
AND
FORESKINS

OF FINGERS AND FORESKINS

Hugh de Lusignan, veteran of thirty-four years of bitter wars and bloody tournaments, was a worried man. A thoughtless remark to a man twisted with grief, and here he was, on his knees before the holy crucifix, praying for holy intervention in a joust way beyond his capabilities.

Eight nights ago he had turned to Sir Geoffrey de Grailly as they both sat at High Table with their Lord, Charles Villouin, Duke of Clairvaux, and let the wine he'd imbibed over the evening do the talking.

"Thy lady wife died alone, I hear tell, Geoffrey. A wretched death. Could thou not spare time from thy whoring to kiss her goodbye?"

The table—nay, the entire hall—had stilled.

Geoffrey had stared at him, rigid with shock and insult. Then he'd lurched to his feet. "Before all here assembled you dare blacken my wife's memory and my name with your foul tongue! Will you let God judge my innocence, Sir Hugh?"

Duke Charles had leaned forward then, his eyes narrowed and careful. "Sir Geoffrey, perhaps—"

"I agree!" Hugh interrupted, banging his wine goblet on the table. "Let God judge."

And now God would. In holy joust, before their Duke and sundry other barons, counts and knights who had attended the banquet and thought now to stay on for the added entertainment.

Hugh's manor house, as solid and dependable as its master, lay only an hour's ride from the Duke's castle, and there Hugh had retired to prepare as best he could.

Now Hugh rose to his feet, using the altar rail to help limbs stiffened with hours of prayer. The chapel was cool and deserted; his wife, Isolde, had kept children and servants far distant to give Hugh the peace he needed. He crossed himself, invoking the name of the Holy Virgin thrice over, then raised his head, staring at the begemmed cross hanging on the wall behind the altar.

Sir Geoffrey de Grailly was a man in the prime of his life, twenty years younger than Hugh. He was a knight of renowned skill and greater courage, and Hugh had been foolish beyond measure not only to insult the man, but then to accept his challenge.

But had not Matilda de Grailly died screaming in childbed? Screaming for a husband who preferred some loose-limbed wanton to his wife's dying?

God would judge, and Hugh was a devout man. God would surely judge in Hugh's favour.

But some holy assistance would be advisable.

Hugh crossed himself one last time and stepped behind the altar to the cross. Reverentially he laid a finger to the secret catch. Few knew that the hollow interior of the cross held a sacred relic: the forefinger of St Guileford himself. With such an exalted relic secreted beneath his armour, Hugh knew he need fear no man.

The withered digit had been handed down from generation to generation, ever since an ancestor had stooped by the saint's body and sliced the memento free. Guileford was a missionary monk who'd died in a hail of stones from a crowd of ungracious pagans who had no stomach for conversion; Hugh's ancestor had been in no doubt that the man would eventually be canonised. For hundreds of years the blessed relic had granted victory in battle to the de Lusignan men, and ease in childbed to their women.

As it would grant Sir Hugh victory on the morrow.

The catch sprung open, revealing the secret space.

Hugh halted, horrified, his hand suspended mid-air.

The space was empty.

"Isolde!" he thundered. *"Isolde!"*

She had been close, awaiting his need, and she rushed to his side. "Sir husband? What ails thee?"

"The relic!" he whispered, unable, in his horror, to say more.

Her dark eyes flitted to the empty cross, then back to her husband's face. She licked her lips. "Husband," she began, "when our eldest lay so ill with the sweating sickness . . . he seemed to be dying . . . and the physicians could do naught . . ."

"Wife . . . *what have you done?*"

"I donated the blessed finger of St Guileford to the good monks of Montegrio, husband. I thought God and His Saints in Heaven would surely listen to my prayers after such an act."

Hugh opened his mouth to shout, but Isolde straightened her shoulders and tilted her chin. "And did not the youth survive, husband? Was not the loss of St Guileford's finger worth our son's life?"

Hugh closed his mouth with a snap and stared at Isolde. Her hair was as dark and her skin as fine as the day he'd first taken her to wife and, despite her small dowry and undoubted temper, he'd never regretted his choice.

But to dispose of St Guileford's finger in so craven a manner?

"You have gone too far, wife!" Hugh snapped. "The relic was not yours to dispose of!

"I—"

"Begone, Isolde." He waved her away irritably. "I need more time in prayer if I am to defeat Sir Geoffrey on the morrow."

"Perhaps if I might suggest—"

"Begone!" Hugh shouted.

Isolde's mouth thinned, but she left without another word.

Hugh sank down to his knees again, deep in thought rather than prayer. How could he defeat Geoffrey if he did not have a sacred relic to catch God's eye? Hugh began to sweat, even in this dim coolness. Where to obtain a suitable relic at this stage?

He bowed his head and closed his eyes, thinking furiously. The de Graillys had long held St John the Baptist's foreskin, and no doubt Sir Geoffrey would sling it about his neck for the joust. What could *he* obtain to counter such holy magic?

Hugh's eyes flew open and he stared unseeing at the stone flagging. When he was a youth he'd witnessed a knight who'd gone a-jousting with his armour fluttering with tiny pieces of parchment, each with a verse from the Holy Bible writ upon it.

Literally armed with God's Word, the knight had unhorsed his opponent on the first pass.

Hugh smiled and struggled to his feet. Several dozen verses from the Bible would surely catch God's eye.

He strode from the chapel, waving Isolde aside. This was something he must do himself. Only if his hand penned the verses would they stand a chance of defeating the Baptist's foreskin.

An hour later he sat in his wife's writing chamber, his fingers smudged uselessly with ink, his brow furrowed in frustration, ignoring Isolde's gentle knocks at the locked door.

Sir Hugh was a fighting man. He'd spent his life battling reckless bandits, invading Germans and vicious Moorish raiders. He had been trained in the arts of war, not the clerkly arts of writing. Hugh *could* read and write, but he found it a bothersome business. He'd found a spare parchment easily enough—he'd ripped it from the back of one of Isolde's account books—as he had a quill and vial of ink. But then Hugh had struck a problem.

His household had no Bible. Bibles were holy and expensive, and normally only the highest of nobility could afford to purchase one from a monastery. The nearest Bible undoubtedly rested in Duke Charles' chapel, but Hugh had neither the wish nor the time to ride to his castle and announce his desperation to the watching world.

So now he sat, trying to recall a verse—any verse—from the Holy Bible. But Hugh had paid as much attention to sermons as he had to his mother's writing lessons. The only verse he could recall, if verse it could be called, was the commandment, "Thou shalt not kill". And somehow Hugh did not think that particular phrase would help him overmuch in a joust where he hoped to do exactly that.

"Holy Virgin, save me," he wrote laboriously on a strip of parchment, then folded it in three.

But several dozen of "Holy Virgin, save me," would do nought against Geoffrey's muscular anger and the Baptist's foreskin.

Hugh sat back in the chair and stared about the room, trying to think. He rarely came here. Isolde, with the help of the steward, attended all the accounts and wrote what letters needed to be penned. It was her room, through and through, furnished to her tastes. Hugh's eyes drifted aimlessly . . . and then stopped, transfixed.

Under the window was a small, unadorned wooden chest. It had arrived in his manor house with Isolde herself, and she'd told him that her father, a renowned Crusader, had brought it back from the Holy Lands. Then Hugh had not been overly curious, more intent on exploring Isolde's body than her furniture, and over the years he'd forgotten the chest's existence.

From the Holy Land? *What if it contained some dust or fragment that Christ himself had touched?*

Hugh dropped to his knees before the chest, and lifted its lid with trembling hands. It was stuffed with numerous irritating trifles—an embroidered cloth, several half-burned candles, incense holders, some vials of unknown liquids and scents—but right at the bottom Hugh found a heavy book.

A Bible?

His heart thumping, Hugh drew it out. It was bound in plain calfskin with a single, mysterious character embossed on its cover.

It must *be holy*, Hugh thought, and opened it up.

He frowned, perplexed. Instead of text, the pages were covered with thousands of tiny, scratchy symbols.

"Hugh?" Isolde whispered through the door. "What is it you do in there?"

The book jumped in his hands. "I study the accounts, wife!" Hugh shouted. "As is my right!"

Her fingers scratched one more time at the door, but she said no more.

Hugh studied the book. Undoubtedly it had come from the Holy Land with the chest. His fingers tapped the pages. What kind of strange writing *was* this?

Then he stilled, remembering the night he'd spent at a monastery long ago. He'd been on his way to war, and the monks, as was their duty, had put him and his retinue up. Of course, their low chattering had bored him witless, and he'd drunk far more than he should . . . but he *did* remember one monk explaining to him how the Holy Gospels came to be recorded. "The founding saints themselves penned them," the monk had said, "writing in the language of Greeks, as was civilised then. Yet Greek is a disturbing language to read, for the ancients wrote with strange characters more like pictures than the Christian alphabet."

Hugh took a deep, incredulous breath, and his eyes widened. *Was he holding one of the original gospels?* Writ by one of the early saints himself in ancient Greek symbols? Brought back to Christendom by Isolde's father?

"By the Saints in Heaven," Hugh whispered. "I must be holding the Gospel of . . ." he thought hard, trying to remember the name of one of the Holy Books, then finished triumphantly, "Luke!"

He closed the book with a snap, and held it to his chest, his eyes shining with adoration. "Holy Father, bless Thee for this sign of Thy beneficence." He kissed book three times. "St Guileford, bless *thee!*"

For was it not St Guileford who had directed this sacred relic into the de Lusignan household?

Back at the writing table, Hugh took quill in hand and proceeded to copy out several verses. Surely the original Gospel of Luke could negate *any* holy magic Geoffrey could command! A-flutter with the Word according to Luke, nothing would dent him!

But the symbols were strange and Hugh's hand cumbersome, and after a few minutes he cursed and threw the quill to one side. Who knew what verses he copied out anyway? No . . . there must be a better way.

For a long time Hugh sat there, thinking. Then he smiled.

Isolde stepped back as the door opened abruptly. "Husband? What hast thou been doing?"

"Thinking, wife," Hugh said. "And casting my eye over the accounts. I find I must take the steward to task. The mill does not grind as it should."

And with that he was off, striding down the stairwell with a strange crackling that floated behind him like a ghostly laugh.

Isolde stared after him, then quickly scanned her writing chamber. Her eyes rested briefly on the chest under the window, but it was closed and calm, and all seemed secure.

Hugh spent a restful night, abstaining from lying with Isolde, for such fleshly delight would corrupt his purity of thought. He rose in the pre-dawn darkness and spent an hour on his knees before the altar in the chapel. He refused to break his fast, taking only sips of water, then asked Isolde to summon his squire, Thomas.

"And leave us be, wife. Women will only tarnish the armour with their touch. Await me in the courtyard."

Thomas was a hearty lad, tall and broad of shoulder and beam. He'd squired Hugh these past five years, and once he'd been sufficiently blooded in battle—and presuming he survived the blood—Hugh would ask Duke Charles to knight him.

But for now all he had to do was murmur encouragement, and lift the armour into place.

Hugh had washed, trimmed his grizzled beard, and now stood waiting Thomas' attentions in linen underclothes and silken hose.

But as Thomas moved to the stand which held the armour, Hugh held up a hand.

"Wait, lad. I wish you to help me with something else first."

Curious, Thomas watched Hugh retrieve a linen-wrapped bundle from beneath the bed. It crackled slightly as Hugh deposited it on a table and proceeded to unwrap it.

Thomas frowned. Sir Hugh had revealed a pile of loose pages. "What . . ?"

Hugh lifted the topmost page and held it reverentially. "'Tis the Holy Word, Thomas. St Luke's *own* Gospel. Writ with his holy hands!"

Hugh had decided that the entire Gospel would provide the best protection and aid. So he'd carefully cut each page from its binding, vowing that once the joust was won he'd have them rebound. Surely St Luke would understand.

Now he waved the page at Thomas. "Holy protection, lad. These pages I shall slip beneath my armour and they will protect me from the evil of dishonour even as they strengthen my sword arm with righteousness!"

Hugh's eyes glowed with strange power as he spoke, and Thomas hurriedly crossed himself. By the Holy Virgin! His master would ride with the Saints this day!

As Thomas assisted Hugh into his armour, he slipped a page or two beneath each piece. God was good, for there was enough of the holy manuscript for it to cover Hugh's entire body, even his legs and arms, as it lay between the linen and the metal plate. There was even a page left to line the helmet.

"Sweet Guileford guide me," murmured Hugh as Thomas lowered the helmet.

He was an imposing sight.

Isolde fretted in the courtyard, pacing to and fro, to and fro before the waiting horses. To one side Hugh's destrier loomed over her and seemingly cast a shadow over the entire day. Silent servants waited with their mistress, their stillness a counterpoint to her nervous anxiety.

Hugh, oh Hugh, she fretted. Why didst thou insult Geoffrey in such a manner? He loved Matilda true, and has suffered twice and twice over since she died. Now you face a man twice your strength who thinks to blunt his grief with your death. Hugh, why cast your life aside with such abandon? Dost thou not realise I love you too great to let you go?

Isolde was caught in a cruel dilemma. Hugh was a devout Christian man and had no idea that his wife worshipped stranger gods than those that were born to virgins and died on crosses. Yet if Isolde beseeched aid from her gods, then how would Hugh's

Christian God react? How would *Hugh* react?

She stopped her pacing and looked up to the tiny window of her writing chamber. There lay Hugh's salvation, if he but knew it. But did she dare use it?

There was a rattle in the archway, and Hugh emerged, Thomas at his back. A servant hurried to lead his warhorse to the mounting block, and Isolde hurried with it.

"Husband," she whispered, her hand on his chest plate. "May the Saints in Heaven smile on you this day."

It was the blessing he would want to hear.

Hugh smiled at her. He felt invulnerable, stronger than he had in many a long year. "Peace, Isolde. Right is on my side. Come now, ride with me to the jousting field and light the way with your gracious smile."

Isolde glanced up at the window again. She could do far more for Hugh here than at the joust. "No," she said, drawing back. "I . . . I feel unwell. I will await you here."

Hugh's eyes darkened with anger and hurt. "As you will, madam. As you *prefer*, madam!"

"Hugh—"

But Hugh had already turned away, allowing Thomas to assist him into his saddle.

The destrier sidled impatiently as he felt his master's weight settle amid a faint crackling.

"I am shamed you do not feel able to accompany me, wife," Hugh said bitterly, then slammed the visor of his helmet shut.

Isolde blinked back tears. She would heal his hurt when he came home safe. But better he come home with an injured heart and alive than with a heart still in death.

"Be safe, husband," she whispered as Hugh wheeled the horse away, Thomas fast behind him on a rangy gelding. A small contingent of men-at-arms clattered after them.

Isolde watched her husband ride away for a few heartbeats, then she hurried inside. Once inside her writing room, she slammed and locked the door, then knelt before the chest. Her hands shaking in impatience and fear for her husband, Isolde lifted out the altar cloth and candles, sprinkling incense and scent about the chest in a sacred circle. Then she reached for the Book of Summons . . . and found nothing but an empty cover.

"Oh merciful Imp!" Isolde cried. "What has he done?"

The sweet-grassed meadow land lay encased by a great sweep of the river as it curved about Villouin Castle. Colourful pavilions had been erected for the ladies and great lords, and they were now full of silken rustles and whispered conversations. Sir Hugh de Lusignan had been a great man in his prime, and still respected, but could he best the brilliant Sir Geoffrey de Grailly? Would one name be wiped completely from heraldic records this day, or would one woman be left widowed?

Geoffrey waited at the end of the lists. His armour was enamelled a brilliant crimson, his destrier draped in gold. Today he meant to restore the honour of his own name and that of his beloved Matilda.

Yes, she had died without him there, and Geoffrey had spent weeks in contrition. But all he felt now was a sense of relief. Today God would judge the guilt . . . if guilt there was.

A murmur ran through the crowds, and Geoffrey looked up.

Sir Hugh had arrived. He waited at the other end of the lists, his metal a-gleaming, his squire and men-at-arms behind him.

Geoffrey's lips stretched in a cold smile. Sir Hugh was a man long past his best—even his destrier bulked more with fat than muscle.

Geoffrey nudged his horse forward at the same moment as Hugh, and the two knights rode slowly towards each other, the only sound the clink of their horses' bits as their heads dipped and swayed with the rhythm of their gait.

They met in the middle of the lists before the Duke's pavilion. Overhead fluttered the pennants of a hundred noble households; underneath the spring grass lay trampled; between the two knights lay cold ill will.

The entire crowd was still.

Both men had the visors of their helmets raised. Hugh's eyes slipped to the neckline of Geoffrey's bright armour. "Dost thou wear thy relic, Sir Geoffrey?"

Geoffrey gave a curt nod, and fingered a small green pouch hanging by a thread about his neck. "The Baptist rides with me this day, Sir Hugh. But I hear rumour St Guileford's finger was sacrificed to save thy son's life a year ago or more."

It was a ritual beginning, the testing of the power of the other's relics, and Geoffrey allowed a small smile of triumph to play about his mouth. He knew naught but Christ's blood itself could beat the might of the Baptist's foreskin.

"I ride wrapped in the might of God's Word as interpreted by the holy Saint Luke," Hugh replied, and Geoffrey blinked at the assurance radiating from the man.

From the pavilion Charles, Duke of Clairvaux, stood forth. "Good sirs," he called, clear and sweet. "Dost thou stand ready?"

"Aye," both knights answered with strong voices.

"Dost thou trust to the judgment of God in this matter?"

"Aye!"

The Duke raised a square of white silk. "Then let the joust commence!"

The knights spared each other one more hostile stare, then wheeled their horses about to their respective ends of the lists. There, squires and attendants hastily checked buckles and spurs, and handed the knights their lances.

In the pavilions and among the crowds to either side of the lists, men and women both leaned forward, their faces tight, their breath held.

Charles checked to make sure that both knights were ready, then, his face calm, let the silken square tumble to the ground.

As Hugh and Geoffrey dug their spurs into their horses' flanks, Isolde leaned over the chest and embraced it, a cry arising from her lips. "Summoner, hear me!"

As the horses thundered towards each other, the Summoner paused in his incessant sweeping, and tipped his head to one side.

Trusting in God, St Guileford and the comforting crackle of the Word of the Blessed St Luke, Hugh fought to keep his lance steady and tucked firmly under his arm as his destrier stampeded into fate.

Geoffrey similarly rode, comforted by the feel of the Baptist's foreskin against the warmth of his throat. Beneath the helmet his eyes were narrowed and cold.

They met above the square of silk, the points of their lances straight and true.

They met in a nightmare of screaming horse and jolted bone, of splintered hell as lances impacted square on plate armour, of breath seized by fingers of pain so vicious both men's heads snapped back and then forward, and fingers loosened about the haft of their lances.

But Geoffrey was the younger and stronger, and his fingers re-tightened first. Screaming Matilda's name he leaned his full weight behind the point of his lance and thrust with all his might.

His lance shattered, but not before it had driven Hugh over so far his weight began to pull him further, and his horse slipped, trying to keep its feet.

Hugh clung desperately to his own lance and to the reins of his horse, but he was winded so badly he had no strength to re-balance himself, and as Geoffrey screamed his wife's name yet again, Hugh slid off his horse.

"Ugh!" he grunted, as he hit the grass, his mail and armour keeping him breathless and weighted to the ground. "St Guileford and St Luke, aid me now!"

But St Guileford and St Luke were silent and singularly unhelpful.

Above him Hugh's destrier screamed and reared, his steel-clad hooves plunging and barely missing Hugh. Then he was gone, forgetting all his training, his master a distant memory writhing helplessly on the grass.

Within pavilion and crowd was utter silence. Sir Hugh was surely dead.

Geoffrey slid carefully from his own horse, throwing the shattered remnants of his lance to one side and drawing his broadsword with slow deliberateness. Flexing fingers within mail gloves, he took a deep breath then raised the sword above his head.

One stroke, and his name and his wife's memory would be purged of all dishonour.

Through the visor of his helmet, Hugh saw the shadow of Geoffrey's arm rise. He felt two emotions overwhelm him then: sorrow that he was about to die, and gladness that Isolde was not, after all, here to see this.

But his will to live overwhelmed all. *"Blessed book, aid me now!"* he screamed.

The sword whistled through the air.

And struck nothing. It kept on falling, over and over in great useless arcs, and Geoffrey tumbled after it. About him writhed unknowable blackness, but within it he could hear and feel Sir Hugh, crashing through into hell with him.

"Holy Virgin!" Sir Hugh cried, and Geoffrey echoed the plea. *Holy Virgin! Save me now! Save me now!*

Then, in an impact filled with so much pain both men *knew* they were dead and wrapped in the arms of Satan himself, they struck hard ground.

After a very long time, Hugh shifted an arm. He could hardly believe he was still alive. Everything hurt. His plate armour was dented and crushed so badly it stabbed and pinched his flesh. His head still rang with the impact, and he could feel a shattered tooth at the back of his mouth.

Ah, he moaned. He had too few of those to lose one more now.

But he was alive, and for that Hugh thanked both the Virgin and the Saints Guileford and Luke who had finally come to his aid.

He rolled over and, after some cursing and shoving, managed to sit up. He tore off his mail gloves, then wrenched the helmet from his head and looked about.

His eyes widened in shock.

A moan to his left made Hugh blink and drop his eyes. Sir Geoffrey. His crimson armour dented and dulled, but his sword still clutched in his right hand, Geoffrey rolled over, trying to get up.

His joust with the man forgotten, Hugh managed to stumble to his feet and totter over to his fellow knight, catching at his hand and hauling him upright.

"My thanks, Sir Hugh," Geoffrey gasped as he, as Hugh had done, wrenched his gloves and helmet off. They stared at each other. Both their faces were bruised and cut, battered by their helmets in the impact.

Geoffrey grimaced wryly. "Have I lost or have you, Sir Hugh? Is this death or do we dream?"

Hugh gestured helplessly at their surroundings. "I know not, Sir Geoffrey. But wherever we are, I fear we have disturbed its peace."

Both men looked about.

They appeared to be standing in the ruins of some ancient, abandoned abbey. Great walls reared eighty paces into the air about them, their masonry withered and pockmarked with age. Their length was punctuated by graceful, sweeping pointed archways, perhaps twenty down each length and five across each end. The roof had long since fallen in, and the building was open to a warm, blue sky. Stones were tumbled about the stone-flagged interior of the ruin.

Beyond the archways stretched lawns and gardens, and walks bordered with trees whose branches swept to the ground.

Hugh met Geoffrey's eyes—as bewildered as his—and opened his mouth to speak, but a faint sound behind them made both knights turn as quickly as their abused armour would allow.

At the far end of the ruin was a dark imp, half a man's height, with a great, lumpish head, large black eyes, and spindly limbs. In its hands it wielded a broom, and as the appalled knights took a step back, the imp grinned and continued its sweep of the lower end of the abbey.

"St Guileford, aid us now," Hugh muttered, more by rote than through any considered thought, and the imp jumped and almost dropped its broom.

"*Wrong!*" it screeched. "Very, very *wrong!*"

Geoffrey mastered his horror. "I still have my sword," he said, preparing to stride down to the evil creature and slice its head from its malformed body. But just as he took his first step, a man walked through an archway close to them.

His eyes were shadowed, his step faltering, his breath rattling in his chest. Purple bruises covered his face and forearms, and blood stains down his robe evidenced more hurt beneath their folds.

He carried about him an inexpressible air of holiness.

The imp giggled.

The man saw the two knights and stretched out a trembling hand.

It was missing a forefinger.

"Are you men of God?" he asked, his voice as quavery as his hand.

Neither Hugh or Geoffrey could answer, their eyes riveted on the man's mutilated hand.

"Have you seen my finger?" Guileford asked, now clasping his injured hand to his breast. It still trickled blood

Hugh took a deep shocked breath.

The imp had scurried closer, and it touched the hem of the saint's robe with the end of its broom handle. The saint took no notice.

"See what you have unwittingly summoned, fool?" the imp hissed, its gleaming eyes on Hugh. "You should take care whose name you invoke in the Hall of Summons!"

Then the imp turned its eyes on Guileford. "Begone, old man."

Guileford stood his ground. "I want my finger," he said.

"It's gone," the imp dismissed. "Now—"

"The wrath of God shall descend on whosoever has my finger!" the saint abruptly screamed, waving his hand about and scattering scarlet drops of blood in a bright arc through the air.

Hugh and Geoffrey, utterly unable to say anything, took a united step backwards. They did not know whether to be more afraid of the imp or the revengeful saint.

The imp stared at the saint, then, shockingly, dropped his broom and rolled about the floor, hugging himself in hysterical laughter. His breath wheezed and bubbled, and his claw-like feet scrabbled at the stone flagging.

"She cooked it!" he finally wheezed. "And fed it . . . fed it to . . . he, he, he . . . !"

Hugh opened his mouth to swear by All the Saints in Heaven, then abruptly shut it. One was enough. "Be very careful that you do not mention the Baptist's name, Sir Geoffrey," he whispered hurriedly. "Imagine the hurt *he* has nursed these past years."

"What goes on here?" Geoffrey hissed, completely bewildered, grabbing Hugh by the arm. "What does he *mean?*"

"He means," a woman's voice put in to one side, "that I stewed the digit and fed it to my son. It was all that saved him from the sweating sickness."

"*Isolde!*" Hugh breathed, jerking his arm out of Geoffrey's grasp.

She stepped from under one of the archways, dressed in black as utter as the imp's eyes, her hair free. Hugh had never seen her looking so beautiful or so wild.

"Your son was dying," the imp said.

"Dying," Isolde echoed, her eyes harsh with grief. "Your god"—Hugh winced at that—"and his saints lay a-sleeping. I sought help where I could. And," she hesitated, glancing at the imp, "the Imp advised me to feed Walter the finger. Combined magic: my spells and the saint's holiness."

Spells? Cold grief clutched at Sir Hugh's heart.

Saint Guileford had paled beyond his previous asheness. "*Sorceress!*" he spat.

"You may cease your bleeding now," the imp said mildly. It had stood again, and was clutching at its broom with renewed purpose. "Your appendage has been irretrievably digested. Now, begone!"

And he swept at the saint with his broom, almost knocking the old man over. "Begone!"

Throwing the assembled group one last furious look, and almost tripping over the broom, the saint stalked off, passing through one of the archways. As soon as he entered the gardens beyond he disappeared.

"The Garden of Death," the imp said, leaning on its broom and looking at the two knights speculatively, "lies beyond the archways."

"My husband." Isolde stepped closer to Hugh, but he flinched away from her. Her eyes glinted, and she reached out an angry hand and seized the metal plate over his arm. "You are a fool,

Hugh! What has so addled your wits that you dress yourself up in the Book of Summons?"

And she whipped out a page from between two plates of armour.

"It be St Luke's Gospel!" Hugh cried.

"Oh!" Isolde began, then could go no further, swamped as she was by her combined fury at and love for this man.

"Isn't it?" Hugh asked.

"It be *my* book," the imp grinned, and sidled closer. Hugh, as Geoffrey, took yet one more step back.

"*I* wrote it with my cunning hands," the imp continued. "It is the Book of Summons, and I am the Summoner."

"You stand in the Hall of Summons," Isolde explained, her temper dissipating. "This Hall stands between life and death, and it is where those alive and those dead may meet and talk. The Summoner," she indicated the imp, "attends the needs of those who visit . . . from whichever side."

Hugh's and Geoffrey's eyes sidled to the imp, then back to Isolde.

"When you screamed for aid," she continued, "as Geoffrey readied the death stroke, you invoked the power of the Book, and it brought you to . . ."

"The Summoner," the imp cried. "And my Hall!"

But Hugh paid the imp no attention. "Oh Lady," he whispered. "Art thou a witch?"

"I am thy wife, Sir Hugh. A wife you have loved these past twenty-five years."

"Answer my question," Hugh rasped. "Art thou a witch?"

She raised her head, her eyes steady. "I revere a different god to thine, husband. Does that make me this 'witch'?"

"And my children," Hugh shouted, recoiling from her. "My heirs! Are they half-bred darkness? Or are they fully as tainted as you?"

"How dare *you* speak of taint to *me*," Isolde hissed, "when 'twas *you* who wrapped himself in the sacred leaves of the Book of Summons!" She took a great breath, the veins standing out on her neck. "And did it not save your life when your god and all his saints lay helpless?"

Hugh stared at her, unable to come to terms with her foul treachery to him *and* to his god. *Sorceress!*

Isolde held his stare, her eyes losing their challenge and pleading for understanding.

"I have heard *enough!*" Geoffrey suddenly rasped, and hefted his sword in both hands.

Isolde and Hugh jumped. They had totally forgotten his presence.

"You are witches, *all* of you," and Geoffrey's wild eyes included Hugh in that statement, "and in the name of—"

"Careful!" shouted the imp.

"—all that is right—"

Geoffrey lunged at the imp with the sword, but it ducked and rolled, cackling and gasping. "All that is *right*, Sir Geoffrey? Oh, very good, Sir Geoffrey, very *good!*"

"—all," Geoffrey cried hoarsely, his chest heaving as he readied the sword for another, more potent stroke, "that is right I condemn you to—"

He swung the sword at Isolde, and would have taken her head had not Hugh lunged unthinkingly and dragged his wife to safety.

"—eternal night!"

And he lunged again. This time the imp was ready, and parried Geoffrey's stroke with its broom.

As Geoffrey struggled to regain his balance, Hugh realised he stood with his arm about Isolde's waist, and hurriedly dropped it. His hands reached for his mace, unsure who he should strike with it.

Geoffrey raised his sword again, his face contorted with . . .

"All that is *right*, husband?" A gentle voice called into the violence. "Is that why you condemned *me*, lonely, into the eternal night?"

Everything, everyone, stilled.

A woman had walked through an archway at the distant end of the abbey, and now stood, a garden breeze wrapping her linen robe about her legs. She did not look a day over eighteen.

In her arms she carried a tiny baby, its curls as golden as hers.

"Matilda!" Geoffrey whispered. He let the sword droop until its tip rested on the flagging.

Isolde, tears in her eyes, took Hugh by the elbow and drew him back. His eyes riveted on the distant woman, Hugh did not resist, nor pull away from his wife's touch.

"All that is right," the imp said very formally, "now stands before us. Summoned."

Matilda slowly walked towards them.

"No, no, no," Geoffrey muttered over and over. "Please, no."

Matilda's eyes were great with tears, and her cheeks still ashen with the shock and horror of death. "Why did you let me die alone, husband? I *needed* you!"

Geoffrey turned his head away, unable to bear the accusation in Matilda's eyes.

Her face hardened, and her arms tightened fractionally about the infant. "I could accept that you betrayed me for months with that woman, husband, but I thought you could have been there for my dying. I thought you respected—*liked*—me enough for that."

Geoffrey's voice broke, but he did not look at her. "I *loved* you, Matilda!"

Matilda's voice cracked across the space between them. "And *her?* Was her bedding worth my despair, husband? Was that evidence of *love*, husband?"

Tears now streamed down both the imp's and Isolde's faces. Hugh stared woodenly at Geoffrey's averted face. *Look her in the eye, man,* he thought roughly. *If nothing else, give her the respect that is her due. Honour her now, in death if not in life.*

Geoffrey slowly, achingly slowly, turned his eyes back to his wife, and winced as he saw the pain that shadowed hers.

"Matilda," he began, then hesitated. "Matilda . . . I had loved you since I first laid eyes on you—you were only eight, then. For years I waited, waited for you to grow. When your father finally agreed to consider offers for your hand, I spent weeks on my knees in prayer that he should contemplate my offer, then weeks more thanking God and the Virgin that he—and you—accepted. On the day of our marriage I trembled when I reached out for your hand in the cathedral . . . surely you remember?"

She jerked her head in assent, her mouth quivering.

"Matilda, that night you were so ethereal, so fragile. I could not believe that I finally held you in my arms. And then, six months later, you told me you were with child."

"I remember," she said. "I remember you recoiling half way across our chamber."

Geoffrey slipped to his knees, the sword clattering from his hands, his eyes not leaving Matilda's face.

"Matilda. I was horrified . . . horrified that I had done this to you. You were too perfect, and far too fragile, to face the horror of childbirth—"

"And yet face it I did!" she cried, and the child whimpered in her arms. "My daughter and I lay wracked for three days and two nights, husband. Did you not once think that your presence would have given us some comfort? Aided our dying?" She paused. *"Three days and two nights I writhed awaiting!"*

"Do you think I don't know that?" Geoffrey screamed, his hands extended, his face ravaged with pain. "Do you think I don't *know* that? Oh, Matilda! That first day I stood in the Hall and listened to your screams. I stood for hours, until I could bear no more. Each of your cries tore my soul to pieces . . . I could bear no more . . ."

"At least *you* had the means to escape," the imp said tonelessly. "Poor Matilda did not."

"I had to leave . . . flee . . ." Geoffrey whispered, and dropped his face into his hands.

"To her," Matilda said, as tonelessly as the imp.

Geoffrey raised his face. "'Twas not her body I felt, but yours," he pleaded. "Not her name I cried, but yours!"

"And *she* did not foul your ears or your conscience with her screams of agony and loneliness, did she, Sir Geoffrey?" the imp rasped unforgivingly, poking at the knight with cruel jabs of its broom handle. "'Twas no wonder you thought her the sweeter company."

It gave Geoffrey one more painful jab, then dropped the broom and reached for the baby. Unhesitatingly, Matilda lowered her into its arms, a small smile glinting through her tears.

SARA DOUGLASS ‡ OF FINGERS AND FORESKINS

"No!" Geoffrey cried as the imp cradled the baby close, crooning wordlessly to her.

The imp half turned away, shielding the baby from her father. "She was lost before she had a chance for life, Sir Geoffrey. Perhaps if you'd attended your wife's pleas, she might have found the strength and courage to birth this sweeting. Perhaps all Matilda needed to survive was the surety of your love . . . the knowledge that *she* was first in your regard. Now she *and* the innocent babe are dead."

Isolde stepped forward from her husband's side and touched the baby lightly on the forehead. "She *is* a sweeting, merciful Imp."

Geoffrey dragged his eyes back to Matilda. "Don't you *see*, Matilda?" he begged. "Don't you understand? I blamed myself for your agony and death. 'Twas I who corrupted you, tarnished your purity, and filled you with the child that killed you. I could not bear the guilt of your ordeal . . . and I still cannot," he finished on a harsh whisper.

Matilda ignored his pain, as he had so long ignored hers, and looked instead at Isolde. "The imp tells me that once you . . . "

Isolde smiled, and took Matilda's hand. "I was once a child like your daughter, Matilda. The imp will do for her what he did for me."

"What?" Hugh exclaimed, surprising even himself with the sound of his voice. "What are you saying, Isolde?" He looked as distraught as Geoffrey did.

Still holding Matilda's hand, Isolde turned back to Hugh. "My father *was* a Crusader, husband. He died with a Saracen scimitar buried in his back, caught fast in the hot sands of the Plains of Jerusalem. When news reached our home, my mother, eight months gone with me, went into labour. Like Matilda," and she gently squeezed the woman's hand, "she died in my unsuccessful birth."

"It is so unfair," the imp murmured, rocking the infant, "that such as these die before they are born. It is *so* unfair!"

"My mother passed through the Garden of Death," Isolde continued, her voice almost a whisper, "when she heard the imp summon her."

45

Hugh stared at his wife, then dropped his eyes to the imp, still utterly absorbed in the child.

"The imp told her that she had lived and died," Isolde said, "and that was in the manner of things, but that I had died before I had lived. He said that she could watch me grow here in the Garden, and that when I had reached the age of fifteen, I would be returned to the world of the living, where I could live out my life."

"But your father," Hugh stumbled to Isolde. "I *met* your father! At the King's court, that Eastertide. He was old, and dying, and you were at his side. He was so desperate to arrange a good marriage for you . . . so desperate . . . "

The imp smiled conspiratorially over the child's head, and Hugh paled. "You did not need much persuading to accept the girl, Sir Hugh," it said. "So overcome were you by her smile."

"And what *price* do you demand for your 'aid'?" Geoffrey demanded of the imp, ignoring Hugh's white face. "What further sacrifice do these women have to make for their children's lives? What price must the *child* pay?"

"None," Matilda and Isolde replied together.

"The imp does it for love of the children," Isolde finished. "For love alone."

Geoffrey's shoulders finally slumped.

"And it guards us and loves us all the days of our lives. Without cost or demands." Isolde looked her husband full in the face. "*Its* love does not need to be purchased with fingers and foreskins."

Hugh blinked, then looked away.

Matilda leaned down and took the sleeping child from the imp. Her tears and bitterness were gone completely now. "Would you like to hold your daughter, husband?"

Wordlessly, Geoffrey held out his arms and cradled the baby to his armoured chest.

He began to cry, silently, hopelessly.

A very long time passed, and there was utter quiet in that abbey.

Finally Geoffrey raised his head and stared at Matilda. "What can I do?" he said. "What can I do to make you forgive me? What penance must I perform?"

Matilda knelt down before him and rested her hand over his as it cradled their child's head. "Will you keep me company *now*, Geoffrey?" The silence deepened.

"Will you die for me?"

"Blessed book, aid me now!" Sir Hugh screamed as Sir Geoffrey swung his sword in a great deadly arc. At the last instant, impossibly, Sir Hugh managed to roll away and Sir Geoffrey's sword bit deep into the earth.

Duke Charles leaned forward, his chest tight, and out of the corner of his eyes he noticed that Sir Hugh's wife, the Lady Isolde, stood at the edge of the crowd, her hand to her throat but her face composed.

Sir Geoffrey struggled to wrench his sword from the earth— *By God!* Duke Charles thought. *You'd think it was caught in the pits of hell!*—and Sir Hugh lurched to his knees, his hand to his mace.

Sir Geoffrey finally yanked his sword from the earth, but as he swung to meet Sir Hugh the mace caught the side of his helmet.

Stunned, the sword fell from his hands and Sir Geoffrey dropped to his knees.

"Ugh!" Sir Hugh grunted, and struck Sir Geoffrey another, more wicked blow.

The knight toppled to the grass. The crowd sighed and, as one, leaned forward. The kill was near.

Isolde raised her hand to her mouth, tears again filling her eyes. *Soon, Matilda, soon. Your husband dies a less lonely, if more dishonourable, death than you.*

Sir Geoffrey had fallen to his back. His ruined helmet gaped open, and Sir Hugh; stepping close, could clearly see the damage his mace had wrought.

He hesitated.

Sir Geoffrey's tongue moved over his bloodied lips, and he managed to force a few words. "Please, Sir Hugh, as you honour me, free me to Matilda. Free me."

And Sir Hugh, tears running down his own face, invisible behind his visor, brought the mace crashing down one last time.

As Sir Geoffrey's squire, uselessly trying to restrain his grief, stood to one side of the body, Duke Charles stepped up.

"God has judged," he said, "and he has judged against thee, Sir Geoffrey de Grailly. Your name is smeared with dishonour, and it is well that it, like you, is now dead."

Thomas carefully unbuckled his master's helmet. Underneath, Sir Hugh's face was streaked with sweat and grime—at least the onlookers assumed the wetness was sweat.

Hugh leaned down and snatched the small green pouch containing the Baptist's foreskin from about the dead man's neck.

"Nay, Sir Duke," he said quietly, as he stood up. "Sir Geoffrey's name lives on in honour." And in the summoning, he thought, in the Garden of Death.

The Duke looked at him strangely. Had the rough and tumble of the joust addled his wits?

Hugh met his Duke's eyes. "Sir Duke, I would beg a boon."

"Ask," Duke Charles said. No one had thought Sir Hugh would win through this day. He must be beloved of God and all His Saints.

"Sir Geoffrey was the last of his line, and has left no issue." Hugh paused at that, and glanced at Isolde standing still and dark several paces away. He looked back at the Duke. "I would ask that you bequeath the name, shield, titles and lands of de Grailly to my youngest son, William."

"You would that your youngest bear the name of a dishonoured man?" Duke Charles asked, startled.

"Sir Geoffrey de Grailly had more honour than the manner of his death indicates, my Lord."

Duke Charles nodded. "As you wish. Both name and title are poor enough. No one else would want them." He paused. "And his lands are William's, too. Your claim is a fair one."

And at that he turned away.

Silently, Sir Geoffrey's servants gathered about to prepare their master's body for burial.

Poor enough in luck, thought Sir Hugh, *but rich enough in love.*

Isolde stepped to his side, her face serene, loving her husband for what he had just done. "I am sure, husband, that once William reaches his majority we shall find him a wife to suit both name and title."

He had won, but at the price of deep-torn flesh and muscles. Once home, Isolde called for hot water and linens, and she dismissed the servants and children as she eased her husband into his bath.

On a table to one side rested a neat pile of pages, rescued from beneath Sir Hugh's armour. Despite the sweat and heat of battle, they were unmarked.

"As I tumbled to the ground, the blood rushed to my head and I had a dream," Hugh said as Isolde washed his bruised and bloodied body. "A very curious dream."

"Is that so, my husband?" she murmured, her eyes all for his bruises. Her hands were very gentle.

"I dreamed . . . "

She raised her eyes to his.

"I dreamed of the love a man has for his wife, and how he should never attempt to deny that love."

She smiled, her eyes tender.

"And I dreamed that fingers and saints are worthless when measured against freely given compassion and love," he finished, softly.

They knelt in prayer, Sir Hugh de Lusignan, his wife Isolde, and their five children, before the altar of the chapel.

There was dust lying across the altar.

Hugh muttered under his breath, but his words had more to do with his encroaching arthritis than holiness.

A soft layer of spider webs encased the begemmed cross, and it no longer glowed as brilliantly as once it did.

Sir Hugh sighed and creaked to his feet, beckoning to his wife and children. As his family filed silently from the chapel, Hugh turned to the black imp industriously sweeping a corner.

"Here, take this," he said, holding out the green pouch he'd lifted from Sir Geoffrey's neck. "Perhaps you might like to give it back to the Baptist."

THE TOWER
ROOM

THE TOWER ROOM

Outside the dark tower giants roamed. Winds screamed. Seas shrieked. She sat on her stool in the room at the top of the tower, waiting. Ice crawled down the walls and sparkled in the fine gossamer of her gown. Nothing moved save the soft rise and fall of her breast.

She had been young in the ways of magic, and foolish. She had come to this tower seeking answers, but had been trapped by its enchantment. She did not know that the last word spoken outside the tower would become as frozen to her lips as she was to this stool. And when she had left home that day her husband had smiled at her and said, "Will you be gone long?"

"No," she replied.

Trapped.

Her husband was now a powerful mage, and yet even he could not rescue her, because he did not yet understand this enchantment.

The winds shifted to batter at a different wall of her prison, and the giants ceased their pacing and pounded furious fists into the air. She lifted her head, her eyes burning.

Her husband arrived in his usual flurry of bright power. He stepped to her side and lifted a fold of the icy material from her shoulder with a gentle finger. Rivulets of warmth ran down her body.

He spoke. "My world is still and listless without you. Will you come home?"

Thus he had asked for each of the five hundred and nine years he'd appeared here to her. There was nothing more she wanted to do than go home. Nothing. But he did not understand the word that jailed her.

"No."

His eyes clouded, and his hand dropped.

When would he ask the right question, she thought? When would he ask, "Would you rather stay here?"

But that was not the question a loving husband asked.

He left.

Outside the dark tower giants roamed. Winds screamed. Seas shrieked. She sat on her stool in the room at the top of the tower, weeping.

The bitterest irony of all was that if the tower knew she wanted to go, then it would let her.

THE FIELD
OF THORNS

THE FIELD OF THORNS

I am old now, and tired, and no longer care for the trite charms and politenesses of the aristocratic society into which I was born. Court life is far behind me—now my life is given almost entirely to pandering the demands of my aching joints. No longer do I winter in my Loire valley chateau with its damp, cold walls, but on the sunnier and gentler slopes of my Provence estates. In the late spring I venture north again, journeying at leisure in my well-sprung and cushioned coach, and now and again shouting ill-naturedly at the coachman to steer the horses well clear of any potholes in the roads. At my age I am entitled to the occasional exhibition of peevishness.

I relish the rambling coach journey north, not only for the beautiful scenery of central France, but for the opportunity it gives me to visit with old friends. The journey north this spring was no exception, save that I decided to vary my routine slightly to visit with a man I had not seen in eight years—the Marquis Montplessier, François de Coutes.

François' father was a close boyhood friend, and I came to know François well during his childhood. After his father died ten years ago, François succeeded to his ancestral titles and estates in the

Montplessier valley and I saw him less often. I did, nevertheless, attend his wedding to a beautiful girl called Ailsa some eight years ago. François was enchanted with his bride, and I was happy for him, and when a year later news arrived that Ailsa had died in a tragic accident I wept a little, and sent François my condolences . . . but I avoided visiting with him in his sorrow.

I have always found grief difficult, and at my age prefer to find excuses rather than deal with grown men weeping.

But I decided that François should be over his loss by now, and I could safely visit. Perhaps we could wile away the days with chess while sampling the giddy wines produced on his valley estates. Perhaps François had even taken another woman to wife, and I could leer at her over the rim of my wine glass.

Old age has its rewards.

Thus it was I urged my coachman towards the Montplessier valley and the ancestral castle of the de Coutes, and fondly dreamed of the reception I would find there.

It was not quite as I had hoped.

My first inkling that all was not as it should be was on the drive through the valley. This was a fertile and rich part of France, and this the most exuberant season of the agricultural year, but as we drove deeper into the valley I saw cottage after cottage either deserted or let to rack and ruin as if its inhabitants no longer cared whether or not the rain swept in through the cracks in the roof. There were peasants in the fields, true, but far fewer than I had remembered, and their labour was lacklustre, and their efforts apathetic.

Most of the fields were left untended, the spring crops left unsown, and the roadways and paths were heavy with weeds.

My unease grew. Had François died himself, and the news not reached me? What else could explain the degree of indifference I witnessed on his estates?

François de Coutes' castle sat on the eastern mountain rim of the valley, and, as we neared the road leading up the mountainside, the view from my coach window grew worse. It seemed as if the land itself had fallen victim to some dark malaise—a spreading sickness that caused trees to twist and die and the grasses and shrubs to wither and crumble.

I sat back in my seat, drawing the curtain across the window with shaking hands. I had seen this wasted, haunted countryside once before in my lifetime, and had never thought to see it again.

I opened my mouth to call to my coachman, thinking to instruct him to turn about the horses and drive at all haste away from the castle, but fear had hoarsened my voice, and all that escaped my mouth were a few useless whispers.

Then the coach lurched as the horses began the final climb towards the castle.

"No!" I whispered, but no one heard.

The coachman reined the horses to a halt in the courtyard of the castle, and I heard sharp, hurried footsteps hastening towards the coach.

Its door flew open, and I stared at the wild-eyed, dishevelled man that stood there.

"Hello, François," I said with commendable sanity. "I have come for a visit."

"Then you have become foolish as well as old," François said, "for no one save the dead tread in this hall of lost footsteps."

I tried to smile reassuringly, but couldn't, and so I merely allowed François to help me from the coach. There were no servants about, and I was not surprised. I raised my head to study the castle. It was a massive structure, built generations ago by François' ancestors, its granite walls filled with glinting windows and topped with fanciful turrets and towers. It had been built atop the crags of the mountains that surrounded the valley, and I knew from my previous visits that on the other side of the castle the mountainside fell away for thousands of feet in a sheer precipice.

I dropped my eyes and looked at François. He could have been no more than thirty-one or two, but he looked almost as old as I. His hair had greyed and thinned, and deep wrinkles criss-crossed his brow and cheeks. His chin was stubbled with four-day-old beard, and his blue eyes burned with either fever or fear, or possibly a combination of both.

Footsteps hurried about the courtyard, but neither myself, François nor my coachman had moved.

The ghostly footsteps rattled again, pattering on the cobbles like soft rain.

"Ailsa died with bare feet, didn't she?" I said, and François stared at me wildly.

We sat long into the night, seated at the grand table in the great hall. The hall stretched for almost eighty paces in length, and some thirty in height, and it needed a small forest to heat and light. Tonight all we had were four candles burning in a candelabra on the table before us, and most of the hall was lost to shifting, watching shadows.

And the constant quiet murmur of dead footsteps.

There was food on the table—some three-day-old bread, a little cheese and some fruit—but François barely touched it. Instead he drank steadily from a glass he refilled from an apparently bottomless ewer of wine; I drank one glass and refused any more.

We talked now and then of inconsequential things, but after a while all conversation ceased, and François slouched morosely in his chair, staring only at his wine glass. After observing him in silence for some time, I asked him what had happened.

"She died," he said, his hands locked about his glass, "and now she won't leave me alone. It was my fault . . . my fault . . . I could have saved her . . . but I was not fast enough . . . I couldn't save her . . . I wasn't—"

"What happened?" I said firmly, cutting through his tirade of self-absorbed misery. Footsteps whispered behind my chair, and I felt the chill of their passing, but I ignored them as best I could.

After all, I'd experienced this before.

François jerked his head towards the line of barely-visible windows that filled the long, eastern wall of the hall.

"She was sitting by the windows," he said, his voice harsh, "and thought to look more closely at the view. So she stood, and leaned against the glass, and—"

I waved my hand, silencing him. He need say no more. I could see it in my mind's eye: Ailsa had stood, leaned against one of the windows, and the catch had given way, sending her plummeting to her death in the precipice beyond.

"I tried to catch her," François whispered, his hands now clenching so tightly about the glass I thought it would break, "but I was not fast enough. She fell, and in falling half turned so that she saw me. She reached out her hand, and I thought I *could* reach her, but our fingertips only grazed, never grasped, and she fell . . . God above, my friend, *she was eight months' pregnant!*

I moaned, hardly believing the enormity of François' tragedy. Not one, but two had died that day.

"We never found her," François whispered. "The depths of the chasm . . . " He shuddered, then jerkily raised the glass to his mouth and drained it of wine.

"François," I said, "what time of year was this?"

François frowned, not understanding the purpose of the question. "The time of year? High summer, my friend. The first of August . . . Lammas Day."

"It was a hot day?"

"Aye. What of it?"

"Ailsa was not wearing shoes." It was not a question.

François almost smiled, remembering. "No. She was little more than a child, and had tossed off her shoes earlier that morning, claiming the heat as excuse enough."

I shuddered, and closed my eyes, and then wished I had not done so, for memory filled my vision . . .

I was eight, and my mother had taken me down to the river to escape the heat. We'd come alone, no servants. She'd been merry, almost girlish, and had kicked off her shoes and raised her skirts about her knees so that she could wade in the waters.

But she'd waded out too far, and the current had taken her.

We'd never found her body, and within a month the footsteps had begun to haunt us, and the fields and meadows about the chateau had begun to fail.

It had taken four years before we'd found the one who could help us, and those four years had been all but ruinous.

"How long since she died?" I asked.

"Seven years," François whispered, and I winced. It was a wonder anything grew at all in this valley.

There was another soft pattering of footsteps running down the hall, and François cried out. "Leave me alone! Leave me! God above, *what do you want?*"

I could have told him then what it was that Ailsa wanted, but he would not have believed me. He needed to be shown, and I was not the man to do that.

"François," I said very gently, reaching across the table to rest my hand on his tight arm, "I know of someone who can help you—"

"I have had a battalion of priests in here to exorcise Ailsa's ghost and lay her to rest," he said, "and none have helped."

"Of course not," I said. "It is not a priest she needs, François, but Ragnorak."

I left the next morning after a sleepless night, promising François that I would return in late July in time for the anniversary of Ailsa's death on the first of August. I said I would bring the man Ragnorak, and François only nodded, not truly caring. He'd had a dozen assorted priests, well-wishers and village witches in to visit, all who'd promised to aid him, and all of whom had failed. Ailsa and her child had continued to roam the hall, their feet pattering in tandem up hall and down steps, seeking, seeking, seeking . . . growing more desperate as year passed into year.

Driving not only François towards the brink of madness, but the entire valley towards destruction.

I prayed it would not be too late.

I reached my own chateau ten days later and immediately sent out word for the man I needed. I hoped he would hear. No one knew where Ragnorak dwelt . . . no one truly cared to ask. All that I could do through the next few months was to hope that he had received my word of need.

In the third week of July I set out along the southern road towards de Coutes' castle. The journey was tiring, conducted as it was during the hottest and dustiest part of the year. A combination of age and fear made my joints ache feverishly, and I am afraid that my tongue grew more waspish the further south we progressed. Soon the coachman, as also the valet who rode with me, were hardly speaking to me.

I could not blame them, but neither could I keep my temper silent.

For nine days we travelled, and my temper grew more vile the further we went without any sign of Ragnorak. I wondered if he was already at the castle, perhaps already hard at work in one of the vaulted cellars under the great hall.

Or had he not heard? Would this trip be in vain? Was François to be fated to complete madness by the lost footsteps that pattered around and about the tormented man?

A half day out from the castle I heard the coachman shout, then suddenly rein in the horses.

I jerked aside the window curtains and peered outside.

Standing by the side of the coach was a tiny, wizened man of indeterminate age. His skin was brown and creased, his hair sparse. He wore a strange costume made up of part leather patches, part folds of silk, and an inordinate number of ribbons, buttons and buckles. At his belt hung the tools of his trade, jingling and jangling as he moved from foot to foot in apparent delight at seeing me. He held a small leather bag in one hand.

I'd seen him last almost seventy years ago . . . and he hadn't changed one wrinkle or one ribbon in all that time.

Ragnorak's brown eyes danced merrily, and his mouth split in a grin, revealing toothless gums.

"Ragnorak!" he cried. "I am Ragnorak!"

I opened the door silently, and he climbed in, sitting on the opposite seat next to my valet, who huddled as far away from the strange man as he could.

Ragnorak grinned. "I know you," he said.

I inclined my head. "My mother once had need of you."

"How many pairs?" he said. He was a man who enjoyed his work.

"Two," I said. "A woman and an infant."

He grinned even wider, and I shouted to the coachman to stop being a laggard and to see if he couldn't manage to whip the horses into movement before dusk.

François only shook his head vaguely when we arrived. In the past few months he seemed to have shrunk, as if he'd let go some vital element of life.

The will to live, perhaps.

He didn't even ask who—or what—Ragnorak was. I merely said that we were here to help, and said that Ragnorak only needed a small, well-lit room in which to work.

François nodded, then shrugged, then began to cry silently as he led us towards the castle entrance.

The footsteps assaulted us as soon as we entered. They were loud and sharp, echoing off every wall and through every space. Ragnorak halted as soon as he heard them, his almost ever-present grin fading as he tilted his head to one side as he listened. Then he nodded, gripped his little bag, and hurried off down a corridor.

I let him go. Ragnorak knew what he needed to do.

It lacked but one day to Lammas.

Lammas Day, the first day of August, dawned bright and hot and, I thought as I rose and walked slowly towards the hall, was probably a twin to that day Ailsa and her unborn child had fallen to their deaths.

Barefooted.

There were steps in the corridor behind me, and I turned.

Ragnorak.

He grinned—*did that grin never fade?*—and held up his hand.

I saw what he clutched, and nodded. Then I turned and completed my journey to the hall.

François was already there. He was dishevelled, his hair mussed, his face unshaven, and his clothes unchanged from the previous day. He was sitting at the window, biting the nails of one hand, and his eyes barely moved in our direction as we entered.

Ragnorak sniffed, uncaring of François' misery, and walked over to the great table where he placed the items he'd had in his hand.

They clunked as they hit the polished surface of the table, and the noise finally dragged François' eyes away from the chasm beyond the window back into the hall.

He looked at the table, and frowned. "Boots?" he said.

Boots, indeed. Over the past day and night Ragnorak had crafted two pairs of walking boots. One pair, Ailsa's, were of stout leather and thick soles and yet, even so, dainty and pretty with laces of ribbons. The other pair were of even finer craftsmanship, for while they were delicate enough to fit the feet of an infant they were nevertheless as stout as Ailsa's.

I shuddered, knowing *why* they needed those stout boots.

"Boots?" François said again. He'd risen and walked closer to the table, his eyes now on Ragnorak as if seeing him for the first time. "What is this? Some jest? Have you come to laugh at me, strange old man?"

François' eyes had slid my way at those final words, and I winced. "Nay, François," I said. "Ragnorak is—"

"You have brought me a cobbler, and thought to comfort me with *boots?*" François shouted.

"François—"

"Have I become so miserable that men can only make fun of me?" he shouted again, and then his face crumpled, and he burst into heart-rending sobs.

My heart almost broke with sorrow for him, but I had been on his journey, too, and I knew that no words could now comfort him.

Only Ragnorak, with his peculiar talents, could ease his soul.

As François sobbed, slumping into a chair with one hand over his eyes, Ragnorak walked over to the window, stood a moment staring outside, then unclasped the latch and swung the window wide open.

"It is a long way down," he said, "and they have yet a long way to go."

Then he stilled, and glanced at the sun. It had risen high in the sky—how had so much time passed?—and Ragnorak nodded. "Soon," he said, and looked back to François.

François, still slumped in the chair with his face in his hand, did not notice.

"François!" Ragnorak suddenly roared. "Ailsa and your child need you!"

François jerked upright, dropping his hand away from his face, then looked at Ragnorak. "Who are you to so order—"

"I am the cobbler to the dead," Ragnorak replied, "and if you want some peace in your life, you will attend to what I say. Now rise, and bring those boots to the window."

François stared at Ragnorak, then looked to me. "François," I said a gently as I could, "Ragnorak sent my mother to peace when her lost footsteps haunted my home and fields. Let him do the same for you."

"Rise," Ragnorak said again, "and bring those boots . . . *now!*" He looked outside. "Quick . . . the sun . . . it is almost time!"

François slowly rose, scraping the chair across the floor. He looked to me once more, and I nodded. "Do as he says, François. Now!"

He hesitated an instant longer, then lifted a slow hand, grasped one set of boots, and then the other, then walked over to the window to stand beside Ragnorak.

The cobbler nodded, acknowledging François' presence, but his eyes were now focussed outside.

Very slowly I moved to stand just behind the two men. I had not thought to witness this vision again until my own death, and despite my fear I could not resist just this one extra glimpse.

François, the boots dangling from one hand, was staring at Ragnorak, but the cobbler raised a hand and grabbed at François' arm. He began to speak in a harsh, urgent voice.

"When someone meets their death before their time," he said, still staring outside, "then they must make their way to the next life without the guide who'd been assigned to them. It is a harsh journey across a field so desolate that it will break your heart to see it."

My toes curled within my own tightly laced boots. I had seen the field that extended between this world and the next, and I knew just how harsh it was.

Ragnorak paused, his eyes scanning the view outside the window. "And when a man or woman or child meets an untimely death in *bare feet* then they cannot cross that field. They are condemned to wandering this world, lost and forsaken, *because they went to their deaths with bare feet!*"

I could see that François still did not understand, but there were no words that could grant understanding, only—

"There!" Ragnorak screeched, and François flinched as the cobbler's hand tightened painfully about his arm.

"There!" the cobbler cried once more, and his free hand pointed out the window.

François looked, and cried out in horror.

Instead of the rise and fall of the mountain ridges beyond the window, now a vast, arid field stretched into infinity. Heat radiated off its surface in palpable waves, and small whorls of wind tore about its surface. But neither the field's heat nor the wind-devils caught one's attention. Instead François' eyes, as mine and as Ragnorak's, were drawn to its actual surface.

The field was entirely covered with sharp three-cornered thorns. Those thorns closest to us, closest to the living world, were dark with dried blood.

"She died, as did her infant," Ragnorak said quietly, "and when she went to cross the field of thorns she could not, because she went to her death with bare feet. She has haunted you ever since, crying out for her shoes."

As my mother haunted my home, I remembered, *seeking her boots so she could cross into the next life.*

"With every year that passes," Ragnorak continued, "Ailsa grows more desperate. See the blood on the thorns nearest us—she has tried and tried to cross, but cannot. And with every year that she fails, so does the land about the site of her death fail, and so does despair cling closer to every living thing."

François took a step forward, as if he meant to leap out the window. He had not taken his eyes off the blood-stained thorns closest to us.

"The boots!" Ragnorak cried. "Throw her the boots!"

"Oh, God, Ailsa," François whispered, "forgive me!" And then he hefted his hand, and threw the boots out the window.

It is hard to describe what happened next. There was a soft wail, and the impression of insubstantial white arms lifting high to seize the two pairs of boots as they sailed through the air.

I know I heard François cry out again, and I think that even I said something, or perhaps even sobbed.

And then the vision of the field shifted, and changed, and then vanished. But in that instant that it changed, in that instant before it disappeared, I saw into *what* it changed.

The dried blood on the thorns near to us glimmered and then shifted, metamorphosing from the lingering traces of despair and failure into soft-petalled crimson flowers. And as that instant closed, I saw the flowers spread in a winding pathway through the field of thorns, and I knew then that Ailsa and her child, as my mother so many years ago, had crossed into the next world.

I am an old, old man, and for the past seventy years, ever since I met Ragnorak for the first time, I have always slept, bathed and fornicated with my shoes on.

One can never be too careful.

THIS WAY TO THE EXIT

THIS WAY TO THE EXIT

James Henry Greathead, chief engineer for the City & South London Railway, rose to his feet as the footman showed the two gentlemen into the club's drawing room. He was relieved the men were reasonably well dressed and didn't gawp at the rich fittings. It had been a risk inviting them to the Athenaeum Club, but the club afforded privacy, and before anything else Greathead wanted privacy for this meeting.

The company could not afford the inevitable financial setback if word he had met with the crypt hunters alarmed the shareholders.

"Mr Kemp? Mr Gordon? So good of you to attend." Greathead gestured to the two men to sit, then nodded at the waiter to bring two more glasses of whisky. "I trust your journey from Windsor was without trouble?"

"Quite, thank you," said Kemp. In his late fifties, Kemp was the slightly older of the two men, but they both shared the careworn and pale visages of those who habitually worked late at night at their books.

Or who habituated the dark underground basements of cities.

They were both very still and calm, regarding Greathead with direct eyes, and Greathead found himself uncrossing, then recrossing his legs, before smoothing back his hair.

He hated it that necessity brought him to these men.

"It surprises me you do not live in London," Greathead said, "as so much of your, um, work is here. Why live in Windsor?"

"You can perhaps understand," Kemp said, his gaze still very direct, "that we prefer the tranquillity of Windsor for our wives and children, as well our own peace of mind. London can be unsettling. Windsor has no—"

Greathead suppressed a wince.

"—discontented underground spaces," Kemp finished.

"Quite," Greathead said.

The waiter returned with the whiskys for Greathead's guests, and while the waiter fussed Greathead took the opportunity to study Gordon and Kemp further. They were unusual men, not so much in background, but for where they had gone in their lives. Gordon had been a vicar who had immersed himself in the study of the churches and monasteries of the medieval and Dark Age periods. He quit the Church of England, quite suddenly, in his early forties. It was about that time that Gordon had met Kemp— Kemp had been a private scholar with a bent for the arcane and mysterious—and they had made a name for themselves speaking at antiquarian functions about southern England.

They had an astounding knowledge of the ancient crypts and vaults and cellars, often dating back to pre-Christian times, that lay under London.

They also had an astounding understanding of what continued to inhabit these ancient crypts—the memories, the terrors, and the wandering ghosts and ambitions of men and gods who refused to remain entombed. Greathead was not quite sure what the men did inside these crypts—they never allowed anyone else in while they were working—but they could somehow manage to desensitise them and make them safe for whoever was trying to push through a railway tunnel or a new sewer or water line.

Underground London was not always quite benign, nor were its forgotten spaces always quite dead. Many tunnellers— whether railway or sewer men—had been lost in the strangest of circumstances. Often the only way the railway or sewer bosses could keep projects on schedule—and workers in the tunnels—was to employ the services of Gordon and Kemp.

The waiter left, and Greathead took a deep breath. "No doubt you have heard of my latest endeavour."

"Of course," said Gordon. "We understandably took some interest when we heard Parliament had authorised your project. A new railway line for southern Londoners, yes? Travelling deep under the Thames to connect their suburbs directly to the City."

"It will be the first deep underground railway system in the world," Greathead said. "Look here, see." He drew a linen-backed map from a satchel to one side of his chair, and unfolded it across the table before Kemp and Gordon. "We are running the line direct from Stockwell in the south, up north through the Borough of Southwark, under the Thames just west of London Bridge, then through the city, deep underground, at least sixty feet deep, through to Moorgate. It is a great enterprise."

Kemp and Gordon exchanged small smiles.

A great enterprise, and fraught with difficulty. There was so much which had been forgotten lying in the railway's path.

"It will be a great deal of work," said Gordon. "All that tunnelling, and, aye, yes, I know of your patented tunnelling machine, and how wonderfully it shall slice through the London clay for you . . . but still, a great deal of work. When do you hope to be completed?"

"1890," said Greathead. "The Prince of Wales has agreed to open the line for us."

"That is not long distant," said Kemp. "You are surely already hard at work, and thus—"

He paused, holding Greathead's eye, and Gordon finished his companion's sentence.

"And thus we are here," he said. "You found a . . . problem."

"The City & South London Railway, whom I represent," Greathead said quietly, "does not have problems. We have only challenges—which we overcome with skill and ingenuity. *Thus* you are here."

Kemp's mouth curved in a small cynical smile, which he hid as he took a sip of his whisky.

It was very good, as was this club, but then Greathead had made a fortune with his innovative and daring engineering work on other railways, and doubtless could afford the luxuries of life.

"Well," said Greathead, "we have started work in several locations, working tunnels in different directions, that they may meet up within months."

"What have you found?" said Kemp, and Greathead glanced irritably at him.

"As I was saying," Greathead said, "we are working in several locations. Here," his finger stabbed down at Clapham, "here," now the finger stabbed down at the northern end of London Bridge, "and," the finger lifted, hesitated, then dropped to the corner of King William Street and Arthur Street East, a few blocks to the north-east of the bridge, "here."

Kemp and Gordon shared another glance, and this time there was no amusement in their expressions.

"That is right by the Monument," said Gordon.

The Monument, erected to mark the exact spot where started the Great Fire of London of 1666. It was an inauspicious omen. Later tragedies were often caused by ancient disturbances below.

Greathead sat back in his chair. "I had heard of your work with the Metropolitan and District Lines," he said. "You smoothed over some considerable difficulties they experienced."

"Few people know of our work with the Metropolitan line," said Gordon. "It was all very—necessarily—secretive."

"I make it my duty to know of your work," said Greathead. "Secretive or not, I made a point of discovering the names of everyone who might be useful to me. Gentlemen, I intend this railway to succeed."

Kemp gave a little shrug. "And now you have encountered one of your little obstacles at the Monument site?"

"It is the site of one of the underground stations," said Greathead. "We are naming it King William Street Station, after the street on which it stands. There is already a commodious building on the site, which will serve as the city offices of the City & South London Railway and as the entrance into the underground station. While there shall be stairs winding down to the platforms sixty feet below, we are installing two large electrified lifts to carry passengers to and from street level. The entire project, gentlemen, shall be electrified, even the trains."

Greathead paused, expecting his guests to remark on this extraordinary innovation, but they continued to regard him calmly with their direct eyes.

"Yes, well," Greathead went on. "We started to sink the shafts through the basement of the building six weeks ago. Work proceeded as planned, then . . . "

"You found a crypt," said Gordon. "Perhaps an ancient vault. Yes?"

"We always expected to find *something*, at some point," said Greathead. "London has been occupied for thousands of years, city built atop city. Naturally we expected an extra basement or two."

"The Metropolitan and District Line gave us much work and worry," said Gordon. "Two crypts, one ancient rotten mausoleum, and one rather dark space which somewhat befuddled us for a day or two. What have you found for us?"

"Nothing that whispers," said Greathead. "Just a . . . space."

The faces of Kemp and Gordon relaxed slightly.

No whispers.

"Nonetheless, I warrant it a space that has caused you to suspend all further work on the shafts and summon us," said Kemp.

Greathead sighed. "The workmen broke into it five days ago. Two of them took down lanterns and explored. When they came back up—well, that was when I wrote you to come to London."

He picked up his whisky glass, then put it down again. "Look, we are not far distant from King William Street. It would be easier, perhaps, if I showed you our difficulties."

Gordon and Kemp stood in the twenty-five foot diameter shaft that stretched down from the basement of the building above. It would one day house two lifts, but for the moment they were surrounded by iron reinforced walls, a muddy floor, half a dozen workmen standing about leaning on their spades and pick-axes, and Greathead.

At their feet was a three foot diameter hole, with a ladder stretching down into the gloom.

One of the workmen handed Kemp a lantern on a rope, and Kemp lowered it carefully down into the darkness.

Everyone standing about—Greathead, the work crew and their supervisor—leaned closer.

"What can you see?" Greathead said.

"Not much," Gordon replied, leaning back a little. "It's a big space, though."

"It will save us a great deal of money and time if it is usable," Greathead said. "The cavern is at the precise level we need to build the station. Both I and the board of the Railway pray for good news."

The lamp hit the bottom of the cavern, and Kemp allowed the remainder of the rope to slide down to join it. He looked at Greathead, then locked eyes with Gordon.

A moment later Gordon began the climb down the ladder, Kemp following directly after.

Kemp held the lantern aloft as the two men stood, staring about. They ignored the faint sounds of the men far above them in the shaft, and instead concentrated every sense on the cavern about them.

"It is not . . . 'bad'," Gordon said very softly. "Not like the crypt under Westminster station. That . . . "

That had been pure evil—something small and weaselly and chattery that had inhabited the small chamber since well before Christianity had established its hold on England. Their efforts to remove the lingering malignancy had almost killed them. Even now Gordon continued to have problems on his shin where the thing had bitten him, and both suffered constant nightmares over the episode.

"No," said Kemp, "it is not 'bad'. But what *is* it?"

The space they stood in looked like a natural cave, although the walls and roof had been obviously man-worked at some time in the ancient past to give the rock a smoother finish. It stretched perhaps some forty or fifty paces from east to west, and, as the two men explored, they discovered that about twenty paces from the eastern end it appeared almost as if another cavern, or tunnel, had intersected with the one in which they stood. On both the northern and southern walls of the main cavern archways had been crudely hewn out of the rock, and passageways extended north and south—if only for a few paces each way before rock falls blocked their progress.

In the very centre of the main cavern, at the intersection of the two smaller passages, stood a pale-stoned cross, almost seven feet tall. The top of the cross had been enclosed within a circle, revealing its ancient pagan origins.

Gordon and Kemp exchanged another glance.

"It's a Long Tom," Gordon said, naming the ancient cross in the manner of countless generations of English peasants. He raised the lamp, and both men muttered soft exclamations.

Set into the circle of stone about the top of the cross was a ring of human teeth.

"I have never seen that previously," Kemp said.

"Nor I," Gordon said. "What do you suppose it means?"

Kemp gave a small shrug. "Perhaps they are the teeth of robbers, or bandits, set here to dissuade others from similar pursuits. In all my studies, I know of no other possible relevance."

"You are likely right," Gordon said, then turned the lamp towards the passageway that had once led south. "These side passages have been blocked off a long, long time ago."

Kemp was still examining the cross in the dim light.

"A crossroads marker," he said. "Long Toms always stood at crossroads to protect travellers." He gestured about the main cavern, then at the two side passages. "We are standing on the site of a very, very ancient crossroad."

"London straddles the junction of several of the ancient roads through England," Gordon said. "This," he indicated the main cavern stretching east to west, "is likely part of the original Wæcelinga Stræt," he said, using the ancient Celt name for what was now known as Watling Street. "And this," he indicated the intersecting, narrowed tunnel, "one of the lesser tracks leading north and south."

He looked up once more at the roof of the cavern. "This has always been enclosed—under a hill, perhaps? Or a man-made tor?"

"Possibly," said Kemp. "This area was once riddled with hills and caves, most imbued with some esoteric significance. Gordon, my friend, this place was not *just* a crossroads. You can feel it too, yes? There is something . . . a gentle pull of some description."

Gordon gave a nod. "But is it *dangerous?*"

Kemp shifted from foot to foot, chewing a lip.

"I don't think so," he said after some consideration. "There is nothing *bad* about this, nothing unsettled. It is a passageway, a throughway. Very ancient, very well travelled—if not in the current millennia—but benign. Even the Long Tom, with its strange circle of teeth, has no feel of malevolence about it."

Gordon gave another nod. "I agree. There is nothing for us here to do. No malignancy to expunge, no sadness to purge. Nothing dangerous."

"Nothing dangerous," said Kemp, "so long as the trains travel through. This cavern will be put to the same purpose for which it has always been used. It will be appropriate, somehow. I doubt the cavern will be unsettled by its updated purpose."

They spent another ten minutes inspecting the cavern, then they climbed back to an impatient Greathead.

"Well?" he said.

Gordon and Kemp exchanged a look.

"The line is going through to north London, isn't it?" Gordon said.

"From Stockwell to Moorgate," Greathead said. "King William Street Station will be the first station north of the river. From there the line travels to Bank, thence to Moorgate. *Well?*"

"The cavern below is an ancient crossroads," said Gordon. "You are lucky. There is nothing malignant to remove, just some old rock falls . . . your King William Street Station is virtually hollowed out for you. There is an old cross down there that you might like to donate to some local antiquarian society, but, overall . . . neither Kemp nor myself foresee any problems for you. Just make sure you take those trains through."

Greathead had begun to smile halfway through Gordon's speech—now he was beaming. He shook each man's hand heartily. "Gentlemen, I thank you indeed. You bring good news.

Come, let us climb back to the surface, and we can arrange your remuneration."

Gordon suppressed a cynical smile.

The railway engineers were always pleased to see the back of Gordon and Kemp.

Eighteen months passed. Greathead called Gordon and Kemp down to London on one more occasion in January of 1890 to investigate something near the London Bridge station, just south of the Thames, but that turned out to be even less of a concern than the King William Street Station cavern. While they were inspecting this latest site, Gordon and Kemp asked Greathead about the ancient crossroads cavern.

"The site is almost complete," Greathead said. "The workmen are laying the last of the tiles, the platforms need a sweep, but other than that . . . " He gave an expressive shrug.

"There have been no problems at the site?" Kemp said.

Greathead hesitated for just an instant, then smiled. "None at all! Now, is there anything else with which I can assist you?"

On the morning of 5th of November, in 1890, Gordon sat at his breakfast table reading the morning paper. There was extensive coverage of the opening of the City & South London Railway line. The Prince of Wales had officiated, and a good time was had by all. Unfortunately, there had been some technical problems with the engine meant to draw the carriages containing the prince and his entourage from Stockwell in the south through to the northern-most station on the line, and eventually everyone had to abandon the railway carriages for the more reliable horse-drawn vehicles on the streets above.

Gordon was grinning broadly by the end of the article. He could easily imagine Greathead's embarrassment at the failure of the train engine. *Dear God, what could he have said to the Prince of Wales?* He folded the paper and put it back to the table, thinking that if it remained fine, then later this afternoon he would make the brisk walk through the frosted streets to Kemp's home so they could share a glass of wine and their amusement at Greathead's discomfiture.

But by noon steady rain had settled in, and Gordon put to one side his plans to visit Kemp.

Christmas came and went. Gordon and Kemp spent some days together, but they did not discuss the City & South London Railway, Greathead, nor their visit to the cavern that was now King William Street Station. Largely they left their London work in London: it was one of the best ways to maintain their serenity.

On a frosty morning in early February Gordon was once again reading his paper at breakfast. His wife had just risen from the table, and he could hear her in the hallway, discussing the evening's meal with their cook, Matilda. There was little of interest in the paper, and Gordon was skimming it somewhat irritably when the headline to a minor paragraph on one of the inner pages caught his eye.

Third person reported missing at King William Street Station.

Gordon fumbled in his haste to fold the paper that he might the more easily read the article, then cursed under his breath as he upset his cup of tea over the pristine tablecloth. Hastily sopping up the mess with his napkin, he read the rest of the article.

On Tuesday last, Mr Arthur Bowman, of Hill End, alighted from the train at King William Street Station. His companion, Mr Charles Marbrock, alighted with Mr Bowman, but lost sight of him in the crowded tunnel leading to the exit. He was not waiting at the entrance foyer when Mr Marbrock exited the lift. A thorough search by station staff provided no clues. Mr Bowman is the third person to go missing from the exit tunnel of King William Street Station since the New Year.

That was it. Nothing else.

The third person to go missing from the exit tunnel of King William Street Station since the New Year?

Gordon rose suddenly, tossing the newspaper down to the table and further upsetting the now-empty tea cup. He strode into the hall, disturbing his wife and Matilda, and grabbed his heavy coat from the hall stand.

"I'm going to see Kemp," he said to his wife. "I doubt I shall return before late afternoon." With that he stomped out the front door.

Late afternoon saw both Kemp and Gordon in the train station at Windsor. It had been a cold walk down almost deserted streets, and both men were pale, their faces pinched by the cold.

They stopped at the ticket box. "Do you have a map of London Underground?" Gordon asked the ticket collector, and thanked the man as he handed one over.

Kemp and Gordon retired to the station fire to look at the map. Neither had been back to London in many months but, since they'd read the news this morning, both had a growing fear that they'd need to return very soon.

Gordon traced a gloved finger over the diagram until he came to the City & South London Line. It was drawn in black to differentiate it from all the other Underground lines currently in service, and Gordon ran his finger up the line from Stockwell to King William Street Station.

The line terminated at King William Street Station.

"It was supposed to go further!" Kemp said. "All the way through to Moorgate!"

"That cavern was a throughway," Gordon hissed. "A *throughway*, not a terminus!"

They walked back to the ticket office, where the ticket collector sat looking bored.

It was freezing weather, and not many people had wanted tickets to London today.

"Good man," said Gordon, "do you know why the City & South London line only goes so far as King William Street Station? We were hoping to catch this line through to Moorgate . . . we thought . . . "

"Heard they had troubles with water seepage north of King William Street," said the ticket collector. "Several buildings collapsed over where they were trying to push through the tunnels." He gave a slight shrug. "Stopped work north, it did. Line now terminates at King William Street Station. But if you want to get to Moorgate, then you can walk to Mark Lane Station, and from there . . . "

Gordon and Kemp paid him no mind.

The line terminated at King William Street?

"Why did we never check?" Gordon whispered. "Why did we never ask?"

"And where are the missing people *going*?" said Kemp.

"Pardon?" said the ticket collector.

The next day, just after noon, the two men stood on the pavement outside the entrance to King William Street Station on Arthur Street East. Passengers were coming and going through the great double doors. Nothing appeared untoward.

Gordon and Kemp exchanged a look, then they went inside, purchased their 2d tickets, then walked through the turnstile to the lifts.

They rode down in silence, not meeting any of the other passenger's eyes. As the last time they had descended this shaft, both men had nerves fluttering in their stomachs. This descent, they knew their nerves would not be easily quelled as previously.

From the lift they took one of two tunnels that led to the station platform. The tunnels were some six feet wide and perhaps eight tall, the white-tiled ceiling curving overhead in an elegant arch.

The platform itself was enclosed in a circular tunnel, again white tiled, and lit with the warm glow of gas lamps. Some fifteen people stood about, waiting for the train from the south to arrive. The tunnel continued a little way north of the platforms, and Gordon and Kemp could see a signal box straddling the track.

Beyond that was a blank brick wall.

The two men turned their attention back to the platform area, trying to orientate themselves with what they remembered of the cavern. They studied the twin tunnels leading to the lifts. Above each tunnel workmen had painted chubby gloved hands, each one with its index finger pointing to the tunnel below.

Between the two chubby gloved hands were the words: *This way to the exit.*

Gordon shivered, although he could not for the moment understand why.

"Gordon?" Kemp said. "D'you see?"

"See what?"

Kemp nodded at the tunnels. "These tunnels are in precisely the same spot as was that south leading tunnel we found. You know the one, with the Long Tom lying half buried a few paces in."

"My God," said Gordon, momentarily forgetting himself in his shocked realisation.

"The original tunnel likely led to a pathway leading to a ford over the Thames," said Kemp, "and from there to one of the roads leading to the south-east and the coast."

"Is that—" Gordon began, but broke off as he heard the sound of the train approaching.

It stopped at the platform—a little grey and cream engine pulling green carriages. None of the carriages had any windows—the City & South London Railway Company had refused to pay for glass when there was nothing to see on the entirely underground line.

Gordon thought they looked like green coffins, and was not surprised to see people bundle out of them in a rush.

He'd be keen to alight, as well.

The disembarked passengers all headed for the exit tunnels, and Gordon and Kemp joined them, mingling among the crowd.

They entered the right hand tunnel and were not four or five paces inside it when both men felt a strange tingling. Kemp, a pace or two behind Gordon, lunged forward and grabbed his friend by the elbow. "What—" he began, then stopped in absolute horror as the person in front of them, a young woman in a fashionable tartan bustled skirt and matching hat, simply faded from view.

Both men staggered in shock, then were pressed against the wall as the tide of passengers continued through the tunnel, heading for the exit.

Buffeted and breathless, they were finally left alone in the tunnel, staring about as if they could miraculously find the woman lurking in the shadows.

They paused for a restorative whisky in a pub on Arthur Street East, then they headed back to the station building which housed the London offices of the City & South London Railway.

There they demanded to see either the chairman of the company, or Mr Greathead, the chief engineer.

As it transpired, both men were in and, after Kemp had shouted a little at the chairman's secretary, both agreed to meet with Gordon and Kemp.

"What in God's name were you thinking," Gordon said, not even waiting to be introduced to the chairman, "not continuing the line? That cavern was a throughway, a *throughway*, not . . . not . . . "

"Not a terminus," Kemp finished.

"If I may?" Greathead said. He waved the men towards a group of chairs by a fire, but neither moved.

Greathead sighed. "May I introduce Sir Charles Grey Mott," he said, the murmured "Mr Gordon, Mr Kemp," as Sir Charles stepped forward to shake the two crypt hunters' hands.

The chairman was a tall, elegant man whose very manner seemed to calm Gordon and Kemp somewhat.

"There is a problem?" Sir Charles said. He sat down in one of the chairs, crossing his legs with such grace that it could only have been bred, not learned, and after a moment both Gordon and Kemp took chairs as well.

Greathead repressed another sigh and joined the others.

"That cavern was a throughway," Gordon said. "An ancient crossroads. It would have been safe had the train continued on its journey, but as it is, the train stops, and people have to go somewhere."

Sir Charles regarded him patiently.

"People have been going missing," said Kemp. "We saw another, today. She vanished before our very eyes. Doubtless there will be a report in tomorrow's *Times*. If it is of any concern."

Sir Charles flickered a glance to Greathead but otherwise his expression did not alter.

"There were problems in continuing the tunnel north," said Greathead. "Water began to seep in and—"

"Yes, yes, so we have heard," said Gordon. "What are you going to do about the station? There are people going missing! On their way to the exit! You *must* continue the tunnel!"

"That is impossible," said Sir Charles. "We simply cannot do it. Instead, in April we shall begin construction on a diversionary tunnel that will run just east of the current line leading into King William Street Station, and bypassing the station entirely. The soil is more stable there, and we should have no problems driving the line north. We anticipate that we can be finished by the end of the year."

Kemp opened his mouth to speak, but Sir Charles continued on smoothly.

"You assured Mr Greathead that the space was safe to be used. You said—"

"That it could only be used if the tunnel continued through!" Gordon said.

"I don't recall you saying that," Greathead said. "In fact, I am sure that you didn't—"

Sir Charles raised a hand for peace. "What is happening to these people, gentlemen? I can assure you, it *is* of concern to me."

"We don't know," said Kemp. "They are travelling *somewhere*, but not to the exit they desire."

"You need to close the station," said Gordon.

"That's impossible!" Greathead said. "King William Street Station is our one and only station currently north of the Thames. If we close it then our entire purpose of building a line from the southern suburbs under the Thames into London is defeated. We might as well—"

"Close the entire line," said Sir Charles. "And if we do that then the company will founder, and thousands shall be left destitute."

Gordon made an impatient noise. "You *must* close it," he said.

"There is nothing you can do?" Sir Charles said. "This is, after all, your speciality. It is what we *paid* you for."

Gordon narrowed his eyes at the tone of Sir Charles' voice and began to shake his head, but Kemp put a hand on his arm.

"There might be something," Kemp said. "The Long Tom."

"The . . . *what?*" Sir Charles said.

"There was an ancient cross in the cavern," Greathead said. "Gordon and Kemp called it a Long Tom and told me to give it to some local antiquarian society."

"It might help," Kemp said, "if it went back into the station. It might protect the passengers."

"*Might*," Gordon muttered.

Neither Greathead nor Sir Charles heard him.

"Where is it now?" Sir Charles said. "Greathead, do you remember where it went?"

Greathead looked a little embarrassed. "Ahem . . . it currently stands in the grounds of my Devon house."

"Good!" Sir Charles said. "it shall be no trouble to restore it, then. Kemp, you are certain this will work? We only need to keep the station open eight or nine months."

"I cannot be sure," Kemp said, "but—"

He stopped. Sir Charles and Greathead were engaged in a conversation about how to transport the Long Tom back to King William Street Station, and from there how to explain its presence to passengers.

Kemp looked at Gordon. *Who knew if it would work?*

And then . . .

What exit were the missing people taking?

Mrs Frances Patterson stepped out of the tunnel and stopped dead, her mouth hanging open.

This was not what she had expected to see.

Instead of streets bustling with horse-drawn vehicles and pedestrians, and footpaths strewn with vendors, all she could see for miles and miles was low rolling hills. To her right stretched what she supposed might have been the Thames, save that it was three times too wide, and where there should have been embankments and warehouses, piers and ships, was nothing but waterbirds and rushes.

A movement before her caught her attention.

Three men stood some fifteen paces away. They wore nothing save woven plaid cloaks and trousers. Their faces and naked upper bodies were daubed with blue woad, their long hair was plaited with what looked like bits of copper, and their eyes were narrowed in suspicion. Each of them carried a long spear.

They were not very tall and looked underfed, and Mrs Patterson vaguely wondered if they were prisoners escaped from one of the city prisons. Newgate, perhaps. Or perhaps native Americans, transported to London's docks by one of the tea clippers.

She cleared her throat. "Is this . . . " She had to stop and start again. They were so rude to stare at her in such fashion! "Is this the way to the exit?"

The three men exchanged glances, making their decision.

One of them leaned his weight on his back foot, and hefted his spear.

Sir Charles Grey Mott sat in his office, looking down at the plan of King William Street Station sitting on his desk.

It had been ten months since he had spoken with Greathead, Gordon and Kemp in this office. In the week following that conversation workmen had restored the ancient pagan cross to the platform, just between the entrances to the two exit tunnels. A little sign attached to the cross had said that it was an artwork on loan from one of the county antiquarian societies.

For two months it appeared to have worked. No one else went missing from the exit tunnels.

Then, very gradually, people started to vanish once again. One every fortnight or so, then the numbers began to increase: one a week, then two a week.

Sir Charles had kept it from the press only because of his extensive contacts, a few bribes, and one rather vicious threat made to the editor of London's largest newspaper. The City & South London Railway was only a very new company, still with only one line, and Parliament could withdraw its consent for the company's continued operation at any time.

There could be no hint of what was going wrong.

So Sir Charles and Greathead pushed their work crews as hard as they could to open up the diversionary tunnel. They found, thank God, no further caverns (if they had, Sir Charles thought he may have taken an early retirement to Panama).

Yesterday the new tunnel through to Moorgate had opened.

Yesterday King William Street Station was finally, thankfully, closed.

Sir Charles would have gone down himself to turn off the gas lamps and smash the damned pagan cross to pieces, save he didn't want to have to risk using the exit tunnels.

He sent the foreman of one of his work crews instead, and, thankfully, he had come back.

Sir Charles stared a long time at the plans, then he reached for his pen, dipped it into the inkwell, and in large black letters wrote across the plan: *Closed due to an engineering blunder.*

Then he pushed back his chair, rose, straightened his vest and jacket, and went back to his wife and family awaiting him in Chelsea. He would have a good evening meal, and relax later in his study with a whisky.

It was all over and done with.

The wind whistled across the marshes surrounding the sacred hills that sat on the bend of the Thames. A small village sat close to the northern bank of the Thames, near a ford, and near to where, one day, London Bridge would stretch across the river. It was only a small village, with eight or nine circular huts, most with smoke drifting from holes in their apex.

Just to the east of the village stood a low hill, one of the sacred hills. The hill had four low arched openings that were centred on each of the cardinal directions.

At least, the hill had *once* had four openings. Now all but one of them were closed over with rubble and turf. A group of six men moved towards the entrance, their steps slow, their shoulders burdened with a tall stone cross, its head enclosed within a stone circle.

Two shamans walked behind the six men and their burden, their heads bowed, murmuring incantations. They had carved the cross between them over the past cycle of the moon, working into it all the protective magics they could.

To one side stood the remainder of the villagers, watching proceedings. Their faces were a mixture of sorrow and relief. They had once revered the sacred hill for the mystical journeys it had enabled them to take, but they had spent the past few months in increasing terror at the evil spirits the hill had begun to spit forth.

They watched the men and the cross vanished within the hill, then the shamans after them. The villagers shuffled a little in their tension.

They hoped the shamans were powerful enough to successfully combat the evil spirits.

After a short while the six men returned, their burden left within the hill. They stood to one side on the entrance, eyeing the tools and the great pile of stone and rubble that stood waiting.

Once the shamans returned (*if* they returned), the men would seal off this remaining doorway.

The two shamans stood in the centre of the crossroads, deep within the hill. They were illumed by two small burning torches and the very faint patch of light that made its way inside from the entrance at their backs. Before them stood the stone cross, the Long Tom.

The shamans regarded it silently for a long moment, then the older of them, the senior shaman, stepped forward. He began to murmur an incantation, at the same time running the fingers of both hands lightly over the teeth set into the circular stonework. The younger shaman bowed his head, remaining silent, concentrating on sending his elder all the strength he could manage.

"It is done," the senior shaman said eventually. He stepped back from the Long Tom, his hands trembling with his weariness.

"The evil spirits will not return?" the other shaman said.

"Not so long as this cross stands here to protect the passageways," said the senior shaman. "We will seal the entrance, and it will never be moved, and our land and people will be safe, for ever more. Now, come, let us leave this place."

Once outside the senior shaman nodded to the villagers standing anxiously, to let them know it had been done, then murmured a word to the six men waiting with tools and stone. The men bent down immediately, beginning to shift the stones.

By morning the entrance would be sealed for evermore.

The two shamans moved down to the river bank. There waited an earthenware pot. The younger man bent and picked it up, then unceremoniously broke the pot against a rock and tipped its contents into the water.

Creamy-grey dust and crushed bone fragments—the cremated remains of all the Londoners who had taken the wrong exit— scattered over the water, creating an oily film that slowly moved away from the river bank into the current to drift eastwards toward the sea.

It was not, all things considered, the exit the chubby gloved hands had promised.

AUTHOR'S NOTE

I have long entertained the idea of writing about one of the abandoned stations in London's Underground. I thought I would need to create a fictionalised station for this story, but when I was doing the research, I came across the strange tale of King William Street Station, destined to be closed due to "an engineering blunder" less than a year after it had opened; it was the first London Underground station to be abandoned. I did not need to look further.

King William Street Station still exists. You can reach it via the emergency stairs leading down from a manhole in the basement of Regis House which stands on King William Street next to the Monument. The gas lamps are still there, as is the signalman's box with its twenty-two hand-operated levers, and most of the Victorian white tiles used to line the ceiling and walls. The twin exit tunnels remain, as do the chubby gloved hands helpfully pointing the way to the exit.

I would advise you not to visit, nor to attempt the way to the exit.

STORIES FROM THE AXIS TRILOGY

FIRE NIGHT

They punched through the barriers between the universe and the world, the shock of their passage creating a rent between the universe and the land that never healed.

Star Gate.

The five craft screamed as they exploded into flame, breaking apart and scattering fiery debris over the darkened landscape beneath them.

Yet even though antennae, wings, empty escape pods, fuel tanks and navigation equipment were torn off, the core pods of each craft remained intact, although fatally crippled.

Nothing could control their descent, save the hearts of those contained within.

The creatures struggling with the controls inside the craft knew they would die within minutes, but they were content in their dying, knowing the secrets they carried would remain safe on this world.

This was a world far, far from their origins. Too far for the Questors to find them easily.

It was tens of thousands of years before the ancient Enchantress would be born and would take into her bed those varied creatures she chose to father her three sons. The land was peopled with humanoid races, hunters and gatherers . . . among them the race that would give rise to the forest Avar. They lived in tents across the plains of this land which no one yet had the skill to name.

These died in their tens of thousands as the molten debris stormed down through the night sky.

Some lived in the marshes bordering the great central river.

They died also as the debris and sparking fuel rained down among them and set the marshes ablaze.

Only those who had camped in the warm caves of the mountain ranges and spreading hills survived in any great numbers. What debris struck the mountains bounced, then rolled down the rocky cliffs. Some few did die as the heated material, in its rush past the cavern mouths, drew out all the air within, but most survived . . . if their hearts did not seize up in fear at the terror without.

Among the raining debris came the cores of the five craft. They struck the land with frightful force, their impact radiating blasts of sound across the continent that killed yet tens of thousands more creatures and peoples.

The creatures within the craft died instantly . . . but they had done their best, and they died thinking their best was going to be enough.

Yet if the alien creatures were dead, the core of their craft still lived. Four of them lay dreaming in the foot of the great craters they had created . . . but the fifth . . . the central one, the command craft, struck the land with such force it burrowed deep into the earth . . . and continued to burrow and seek and search until it found the place it needed.

There . . . following the instructions buried within its memory banks . . . it mutated, expanded, twisted . . . creating the goal of its instructions. The City.

At its heart, the imprisoned soul seethed . . . wanting the feel of the midday sun across its back once more. Needing.

Across the land, debris continued to rain down, and it set fire to the land, and it burned for five nights and five days without ceasing.

Bravest of those left, the woman emerged on the sixth day and stood aghast at the desolation before her.

She stood at the lip where cave mouth met cliff, and stared. Stretching south before her lay a wasteland of charcoal and ash. The great river had evaporated—all that was left to mark its course down to the great southern sea was a twisting canyon half filled with embers and drifting ash.

Above the sky was streaked with red and black, hung about with great clouds of fine ash that were even now still lined with smoldering fires.

She dropped her eyes as tears streaked her face. Where the forests? The grasslands? The snake—and frog-filled marshlands?

Where her brothers and sisters who had wandered the game trails below?

Her husband stepped up behind her and put a hand on her shoulder.

"It is all gone," she whispered. "Where? For what?"

His hand tightened, but in his grief at the destruction before him he could say nothing.

They stood, weeping, watching, until he started in surprise and pointed. "Look! There . . . and there!"

She followed the course of his hand. Four great depressions had been punched into the plains, and her keen eyes could just pick out the glint of water within them. Multifaceted jewels and sheets of silver and gold appeared to glisten beneath the shallow waters . . . or was that just a trickery of the newly risen sun glinting across the water?

"Lakes," her husband whispered, "given us as gifts by the gods."

"Sacred Lakes," she murmured, shivering. "This land has been seeded with magic."

Her husband sighed, and slid his arms about his wife. "Perhaps . . . but it is going to be a bad winter."

THE RISE OF THE SENESCHAL

The Seneschal was founded about a knife-scarred table deep in the back shadows of the Twisted Bulls Tavern in Carlon some fifteen-hundred years before the time of the Prophecy of the Destroyer. It began as a nascent political movement around dusk and during the third round of ale, but had progressed to a religious movement of peculiar fervour by moon rise and the arrival of the ninth round of ale.

Well . . . that's the way the current proprietor of the Twisted Bulls tells the story. In reality, the rise of the Seneschal predated that drunken conversation (which actually happened, but five of those men grouped about the table that night never realised the extent of their manipulation by the sixth), and it occurred in far distant Smyrton . . . not amid the indolence of golden-roofed and pink-walled Carlon.

For thousands of years stolid but reliable peasants eked out a living from the poor soils of the plains and valleys of ancient Tencendor. To the west and south lived the magical Icarii and Avar, but the plains held little appeal for the Peoples of the Wing and the Horn, and they cared even less for the subsistence agriculture of the peasants. The humans of Tencendor lived in small villages or wandering groups, raising sorry herds of cattle and sheep, and eking what wealth and food from the soil they could with inadequate digging sticks powered by apathy. These were days when the forests spread over much of Tencendor— even the west of the continent beyond the River Nordra was heavily forested—and the plains were kept well in the shadow of the trees. Crop-raising and cattle-slaying came a poor second to soaring the skies and divining the true nature of the trees, and it was left to the human peoples to provide what grain and meat the Icarii and Avar required.

Far to the north where the Nordra roared out of the confining chasm in steep hills lay a pitiful collection of huts called Smyrton. Here eleven family groups did what they had to in order to survive . . . and not much else. They spent their days dragging their feet through the dust of their two fields or wandering behind their thin-ribbed herds of cattle, they spent their nights huddled silently about fires, and day and night their minds ranged vacant . . . and vulnerable.

One dull autumn day the Goodman from family Hordley was shuffling his way down the path between summer field and winter field towards Smyrton. His back ached, several small blisters on his left hand had broken open, one had a splinter in it, and his upper left molar was pounding with the pressure of the abscess above it. Hordley hoped his wife had stewed the turnips well this night, for he did not feel like chewing overly long about them if she hadn't.

And if she *hadn't* stewed them well enough, then perhaps he would beat her—just a little—to make sure she did her task well enough the next time.

His left hand twitched, and his mouth twisted, anticipating.

His foot caught against a stone, and Hordley stumbled and almost fell. He cursed low and foul, invoking the black words associated with blood and death, and the idea that he should beat his wife in any case firmed into near certainty in his mind. It would do her good. And it might well relieve the frustration of his tooth . . . nay, of his entire life.

Hordley pulled his tattered cloak a little closer against the sharp northerly wind and strode ahead with renewed purpose, narrowing his eyes into the dusk. After a few steps he halted, unsure. Feeling the change . . . the presence . . . but not understanding what it could be. Then he slowly turned about.

Something was coming up the path behind him. Hordley peered . . . and the pain of his tooth vanished abruptly as he saw what approached. He tried to run, but couldn't find the will to accomplish it. He whimpered, and drooled terrified and slightly blood-stained spittle down his chin.

There were beasts advancing upon him. Two great cattle bulls, white, red-eyed, razor-horned and hooved. Their heads tossed wildly, furiously, their hooves pounded into the path, driven by bunched haunches powered by fury.

Behind them thumped and thudded a contraption that Hordley was sure would grind him into the soil. It had wheels that rolled to shoulder-height, their nail heads glinting in the red and orange rays of the sunset. A great beam ran down between the wheels, and in the belly of this beam Hordley could glimpse metal blades and shaped keels that knifed into the packed soil of the path and tossed it to one side.

It was truly a ferocious beast.

And yet none of this was any match for the terror of what drove bulls and contraption. A man, and yet no man. He stood half as high again as any man Hordley had ever seen, and his countenance was more terrible than those of the bulls. He wore a short leather cape, a dirty cloth girt about his loins, and muscles bunched and rolled about his all-but-naked body. Sandals clung to his feet, and there was a goad in one hand that the . . . man? . . . now raised threateningly above one shoulder.

The bulls screamed.

Hordley screamed with them, his jaw quivering with such horror his abscessed tooth gave way and sprayed out in blood- and pus-flecked ivory shards across the path.

The bulls were now so close the heat from their eyes burned his face, but Hordley still could not move.

"You will gather your companions about," said the power behind the wheels.

"Yes," Hordley whispered.

"You will listen to what I have to say."

"Yes."

"I bring you joy." Hordley believed it, but he found himself unable to answer.

"And I bring you power."

Hordley smiled.

And so Artor the Ravener spoke to the good folk of Smyrton, and set them on their long road into Hell. He spoke to them of the contraption His bulls pulled, and it was named Plough. It would give them straight lines and square fields, He promised, and it would eventually give them power.

Every one of the villagers smiled.

And Artor the Ravener was so pleased with the good villagers of Smyrton He presented them with the Book of Field and Furrow so that they might the more readily interpret His wishes and obey His commands.

"For I am Artor," He said, "and I raven."

Hordley clutched the Book to his breast. "How might we serve you, Artor?"

"By ploughing the earth and preparing the way," Artor replied, "so that one day I might multiply."

"We shall spread the word and cause a Plough to be built in every village and glade, Artor."

"And you shall build an edifice to house My name and My will."

They were silent, puzzled.

"You shall call it the Seneschal, and it shall watch over the hearts and souls of those who cling to My Plough."

"Ah," Hordley breathed. "As Your will dictates, Mightiness."

Artor came as close to smiling as he could. "Furrow wide, My good people, furrow deep."

So it was that after the villagers of Smyrton had struggled with the Plough for nigh on six months and learned of its ways, they sent one of their sons, Egerly, on the long journey down to the lands of the far south to garner more souls for the pleasure of Artor and the Way of the Plough. Egerly took with him many plans, some on parchment—and these he showed in villages as he went south, praising this strange new device called a Plough—

and many in his mind, and these he disseminated more subtly with the help of his god, Artor.

The Way of the Plough was fruitful. It spread from the villages and the sorry wandering groups to whom Egerly had taught the uses of the device Plough, and it spread from the Twisted Bulls tavern in Carlon, where Egerly had first gathered to him the seeds of the Brotherhood of the Seneschal—he its first Brother-Leader.

The Way of the Plough spread like a smoldering fire across an unguarded hearth, fingering at the hearts of a people who had always felt inferior to the bright feathered Icarii and the shadowy Avar. Artor and His Way of the Plough gave them hope, hope that one day they might best the Icarii and dispossess the Avar. Hope that one day they could claim the entire land as their own.

"Ours," Brother-Leader Egerly whispered through the minds of his growing band of listeners. "Ours, and we shall name it for ourselves. Achar."

When word of the new faith reached the ears of the Avar, they shrugged and forgot it, for it did not concern them—but then, they had not heard all of what the new craft preached.

When word of the Way of the Plough reached the ears of the Icarii, they did not even deign to discuss it in the Assembly, for they could not recognise the threat, and they laughed that the stolid humans should even aspire to a faith.

"The next we know they'll be claiming knowledge of magical crafts," laughed one of the Enchanters to the Talon as they rode the thermals above Grail Lake, and then both birdmen dismissed the subject, not realising the Acharites aspired not to magical crafts, but to their complete destruction.

None among the Avar or Icarii knew or understood of the storm fomenting. None realised that within a generation, the Wars of the Axe would tear their complacency apart.

THE WARS OF THE AXE

The Seneschal grew, garnering power to itself, spreading among the poor of the countryside and the hopeless of the cities. The Way of the Plough spread, and so did the fields, until the ringing of the axes at the edges of the forests made both Icarii and Avar flinch.

GoldFlight SunSoar was then Talon over all Tencendor, and he, like the two Talons before him, had tolerated the spread of the Way of the Plough. They either thought it a diverting amusement, suitable to the Acharites and their stolid ways, or they thought it a useful faith, for this strange new invention of the Plough meant that Tencendor's grain crop increased fifteen-fold within only a generation.

They did not see the danger.

The Icarii continued to play amid the skies, and there sought the answers of the stars. The Avar continued to wander the forest paths, seeking nothing but peace and continued goodwill towards the land.

All this the Acharites saw. The Brothers of the Seneschal, spreading among the Acharite communities like the thin, vibrant trickle of disease, told the people that they should covet what the Icarii and Avar enjoyed.

"Do they not inhabit the best places . . . the choicest? Is their way of life not one of ease and waste while yours is one of toil and pain? Do the Icarii not eat of the best, and recline amid silks and velvets, while you grind your teeth on coarse bread and lie amid the dust of your hovels? Do not the Avar uselessly inhabit dark forests, places of demons and shadows, that might be better used as grainlands? See . . . see . . . "

And the Acharites saw, and were increasingly resentful. And, resentful, they hefted their axes and nibbled at the edges of the great forests.

The Avar complained to the Talon, and GoldFlight SunSoar called representatives of the Acharites to meet with him in his palace in the cities of the Minaret Peaks. Among the twelve Acharites who appeared before GoldFlight and his advisers were three Brothers of the Seneschal. They were the first Brothers GoldFlight had ever met, and he did not like their cold, flat eyes, nor their refusal to shake his hand.

The meeting did not go well. The Acharites, encouraged by the Brothers of the Seneschal, demanded freedoms and land.

"We would that you cede to us all the land east of the Nordra," shouted their spokesman, "and that we be known no more as bondsmen to the Icarii!"

GoldFlight was shocked. "All the land to the east . . . bondsmen? Bondsmen? What do you mean?"

"We are your slaves—"

"No!" GoldFlight leapt to his feet, his wings extended behind him. "Slaves? I—"

"*Slaves!*" the spokesman screamed, the hand of a Brother firm on his shoulder. "We work only to provide the food for your feasts and the fools for your entertainments! You think nothing of us, save to laugh at our poverty and wretchedness!"

"No," GoldFlight whispered, appalled that he, as the entire Icarii, should be so accused. "No."

"Then give us our freedom, and give us the land east of the Nordra. All of it."

"But that land is forested . . . what would you—"

"We would *de*forest it," one of the Brothers hissed. "We would clear the land of its demons and we would put it into the use of the Acharites and Artor himself, may his name be blessed forever."

GoldFlight, utterly shocked, sank down onto his stool. "No," he managed after a moment. "No. What you speak is foolishness. What you suggest is sacrilege. The forest is the home of the Avar—"

"Witches!" one of the Acharites whispered.

"—and neither you nor I have the right to deprive them of—"

"They are black-hearted wretches who shall feed our axes," a Brother said calmly. "Stay out of our way, birdmen."

At that GoldFlight had them thrown out of his presence. He kept them for a month under close guard, but such were the murmurings among the Acharite populations he eventually let them go.

"They truly could not have meant what they said," GoldFlight remarked to his son. "It must have been . . . it must have been . . . Oh! They will forget it!"

And with that he turned away.

For some time it appeared as if GoldFlight was correct. Once the twelve men and three brothers of the Seneschal had been released they returned home from the Minaret Peaks and were absorbed silently back into their communities. For eighteen months there was nothing. Axes still occasionally rang at the edges of the forests, but their activity died down somewhat, and GoldFlight allowed himself the luxury of believing the moment of rebellion was over.

And if it did come to armed conflict . . . well . . . he commanded the Strike Force . . . and the Acharites had nothing to counter them.

Except cunning and determination.

The Acharites, as the Skraelings would later strike during Yuletide, struck during Beltide. Beltide was celebrated across Tencendor, although the Acharites, increasingly under the influence of the Seneschal, generally largely ignored it. Not this year. As the Avar and the Icarii followed the pathways chosen them by their lust, as they lay down entwined among the trees and in the glades of the great forests, silent assassins moved among them. Knives struck where love only should have ventured, spears pierced passion, and axes clove couples apart.

Leading the Acharites were a thousand men dressed in grey, their leader in black, twin crossed axes on his breast. Secretly formed by the Seneschal more than two years previously, and trained amid even more secrecy, the Axe-Wielders struck efficiently and without mercy. As other Acharites slaughtered indiscriminately if enthusiastically, the BattleAxe directed his Axe-Wielders against Crest- and Wing-Leaders, and Clan Heads among the Avar.

The Icarii and Avar were decimated . . . not only in numbers lost (and legend claims that twenty-thousand among them died that Beltide night) but in leadership and courage and heart for the fight. The Strike Force was virtually useless. They did not know how to battle against thieves in the night, nor did they understand how to battle the determination of those determined to clear the skies above . . . Achar.

Supported by the now triumphant Seneschal, a baron named Tristian claimed the crown of the new nation of Achar. Buoyed by their Beltide success, thousands of peasants flocked to fight under the direction of the Axe-Wielders and their BattleAxe. The Icarii and the Avar were shell-shocked. None among them could rally their fellows against the insurgency. GoldFlight, reeling from the loss of his wife and daughter at Beltide, ordered the Icarii Strike Force back to protect the cities of the Minaret Peaks. The Avar would have to look after themselves.

"Just for a week or two," GoldFlight promised, "until we cope against the Acharites."

But weeks turned into long impotent months, and the Avar fled north, ever north along the forest paths as the Acharites fell to their axe-wielding with a vengeance. Tens of thousands of Acharites, armed with sharp axes, lined the borders of the forests and hacked their way in. Among them strode Brothers of the Seneschal, shouting, encouraging, their voices spittle-lined with triumph. Behind the lines of axemen marched the peasants and their plough teams, carting away (or burning) the cut timber and ploughing the detritus into the soil.

Only about the Silent Woman Keep did the Acharites encounter determined resistance, and then from the powerful magic of the Keep and the surrounding trees and the wonder of what lay in the depths of Cauldron Lake more than from any members of the Icarii Strike Force. Eventually the Seneschal ordered the axemen away from this stubborn patch of trees.

"They will fall eventually," the Brothers claimed. "We will conquer this pitiful patch some day."

And so they moved north, north, towards the beautiful Minaret Peaks.

Icarii cities chiselled into and soaring above the Minaret Peaks were tunnelled and colonnaded in wondrous stones and gems, marbled with beauty, imbued with magic. As the lines of Axemen approached, GoldFlight, his wings drooping with sorrow, ordered the evacuation of his people north. "North to Talon Spike," he whispered, his eyes tracing the approach of fires to the south.

To the Enchanters among them, GoldFlight said, "Do what you can. I could not bear to see these wondrous cities destroyed."

"It will take time," said his brother StarJoy. "Weeks to protect these cities from the evil approaching. Can your . . . Strike Force . . . protect us in that time?"

GoldFlight took the rebuke unflinchingly. "They will have to, StarJoy."

And they did, but it was almost the destruction of them. As the Icarii Enchanters struggled to drape the Minaret cities in concealing magic, struggled to hide their soaring spires and their treasured domes from the darkened eyes of the Acharites, the Strike Force spent its days and nights in the sky, keeping the enraged axemen at bay. Every day more and more of them dropped from the increasingly accurate arrows of the Acharites, yet they kept attacking and, if not driving the Acharites back, at least throwing a wall of protection around the cities and the Enchanters.

"Sorcery!" screamed the Brothers of the Seneschal as each day saw spires and domes fade from view to be replaced by the bare sweep of bracken-encrusted hills.

More than anything else, this display of power and magic persuaded the Acharites that the Icarii, as their brothers in magic the Avar, were creatures to be feared and, being feared, to be slaughtered without pity.

"How long before they throw that might down upon your wives and children?" the Seneschal cried, and men feared.

"How long before they ensorcel your souls with their blackness?"

And the Acharites redoubled their efforts against the Strike Force until only a pitiful few Wings were left. GoldFlight, who had stayed to the last, watched as the last three Wings, each at only half-strength, limped back to the remaining colonnade on their final night in what had been the pride of the Icarii race.

"We leave during the night," GoldFlight said, and with those words condemned the Icarii to a thousand-year exile. "We skulk away under cover of darkness."

And this they did. As the Acharites broke through the remaining defences, the Icarii lifted into the night and winged their way north. Some died from exhaustion—many the best Enchanters alive—and others dropped from the sky in sheer sad-heartedness, but most made it across the Fortress Ranges into the forests.

"Soon," GoldFlight said to the Icarii and the Avar about. "Soon we will regroup and fight our way back. Soon."

Far to the rear of the group an Icarii male, copper hair and violet eyes well hid under a concealing hood, turned away and wept. He knew how long it would take for the StarMan to emerge from the ashes of the Icarii pride. Even though WolfStar had known for generations of this horror, the actual sight of it sorrowed him beyond belief.

"Soon," GoldFlight repeated uselessly, and no-one there believed him. No-one.

The Acharites hacked and they burned. Within ten years they had cleared the forests of Achar from the Fortress Ranges to Widewall Bay and from the Nordra in the west to the Widowmaker Sea to the east. Save the stubborn trees surrounding the Silent Woman Keep and Cauldron Lake, and a few scraggles about the Fernbrake Lake, nothing remained. Shadowed walks turned into sun-deadened grasslands, magical glades faded into memory, the Mother moaned and turned away.

The Seneschal spread stories of the mighty battles of the Wars of the Axe. "The Icarii and Avar, the Forbidden Ones, tortured and raped," they said, and all who listened believed the Brothers, even those who had seen the wars first hand. "Women were dragged from their beds to assuage Icarii lust, children slaughtered to appease their dark gods. The trees walked the night, biting and wrenching Artor-fearing people limb from limb, and forest gnomes stole souls and sold them to demons. Fear their return . . . Fear . . . Only Artor can save you."

So people listened and feared and believed, and the Way of the Plough flourished, and the Seneschal waxed fat on the power of fear, and Artor, the great god Artor, imprisoned the seven revealed Star Gods in an icy barrenness within the interstellar wastes.

And meanwhile the magic at the foot of the Lakes watched and listened and relaxed, for while the battles raged overhead it had feared that the final conflagration had arrived. But not yet . . . not yet.

HOW AXIS FOUND HIS AXE

Axis was born at Gorkentown in the far north of Ichtar, the fatherless, illegitimate son of Princess Rivkah of Achar, wife of Duke Searlas of Ichtar. His mother apparently dead in his birth, and her cuckolded husband refusing to acknowledge the boy, it was left to the kindness of Brother Jayme, a member of the religious order of the Seneschal devoted to the service of the Plough God Artor, to take the infant into care.

The Seneschal protected and nurtured Axis during his infant and early boyhood, providing his only family. Jayme was the closest thing Axis had to a father, and Jayme's friend within the Seneschal, Moryson, became Axis' tutor and confidante. These two men formed the core of Axis' world, and shaped his entire perception and understanding of life. In a world where he was constantly reviled for his bastard origins, Axis found succour only among the Seneschal and in his prayers to the great god Artor.

When Axis was seven, Jayme—who by now was among the very senior members of the Seneschal—suggested to the boy that he enter one of the Seneschal's Retreats to take minor orders with a view to becoming a member of the Brotherhood himself. What else could the bastard of a shamed princess hope for than secure anonymity within the Order? Besides, Axis had a remarkable facility for music and a fine singing voice, and Jayme envisioned him growing into a man who could write majestic anthems and hymns to Artor and the Seneschal's glory.

Until now Jayme had only to say the word for Axis to obey, but, for the first time in his young life, Axis refused Jayme's suggestion.

"I want to become a hero!" he exclaimed, standing stiff and proud before Brother Jayme, who had to repress a grin at the boy's proud defiance.

"I want to defend the Seneschal," Axis continued, his pale blue eyes blazing. "I will do better for the Seneschal with a sword in my hands than a hymn in my mouth."

Jayme's eyes filled with tears, moved by the boy's devotion. Moryson stood at Jayme's side, and he nodded to himself as Axis spoke, as if the boy had just passed some kind of test.

"He will become an Axe-Wielder," said Moryson matter-of-factly, speaking of the elite military wing of the Seneschal. He put a hand on Jayme's shoulder. "And when you become Brother-Leader, Jayme, Axis shall lead the Axe-Wielders as your BattleAxe. Warriors can sing, too."

Jayme laughed at that, but Moryson and Axis locked eyes, and Moryson nodded very slightly at the young boy.

"You shall become BattleAxe," Moryson said softly. "Believe it. A BattleAxe such as this land has never seen before."

Accordingly, Axis learned the arts of the warrior. To begin, Jayme sent him to the court of Jorge, earl of Avonsdale. Here Axis trained first as a page and then as a squire. When he reached the age of eleven, Axis transferred to the court of Ganelon, the Lord of Tare. Ganelon had been an Axe-Wielder until the death of his elder brother necessitated his return into secular life to succeed to the inheritance of Tare. It was Ganelon who introduced Axis to the weapons of the Axe-Wielder, the axe and the sword, and who taught him to ride as a warrior. It was Ganelon's wife, Embeth, who introduced the young boy to the possibilities of love. Possibilities only, for neither Axis nor Embeth took that fatal step into dishonour, but it was enough to mark both their lives.

When Axis turned seventeen, and reached the height and strength of a man, he travelled back to Jayme, who, now the First Advisor to the Brother-Leader, resided at the Tower of the Seneschal on the shores of Grail Lake.

"Father!" Axis said, first bowing, then moving forward to embrace Jayme.

Jayme hugged him tightly, then stepped back and looked the youth up and down. The boy had grown into a fine young man, very tall and as finely muscled as a dancer. He had a strange look about his face, an alien cast of feature, and as he had so often before, Jayme wondered again who had got this boy on Princess Rivkah. "You know," he said, "when you were born Searlas told me to drown you. I am glad I didn't." It was an affectionate statement, but also a calculated one, meant to remind Axis that he owed Jayme a great deal.

It had the desired effect. Axis dropped to one knee and kissed Jayme's hand. "I am yours," he said. "All I want is to serve you and the Seneschal."

Jayme looked over Axis' fair bowed head to where Moryson stood behind him. Many years ago Moryson had said that Jayme would be Brother-Leader of the Seneschal, and Axis his BattleAxe, leader of the legendary Axe-Wielders. Then Jayme had laughed. Now, with the current Brother-Leader, Hoare, growing older and weaker, and himself as the man's deputy, Jayme knew he was in a strong enough position to take control once Hoare died.

And if he then had a BattleAxe who not only controlled the military wing of the Seneschal, but was so devoted to Jayme that he would obey without question . . . well then . . . what could he not accomplish? But first Axis must undertake the ordeal of joining the Axe-Wielders . . . and survive that ordeal.

"I think," Jayme said gently to Axis, "it is time for you to join the Axe-Wielders."

"Yes!" said Axis, now gazing up. "Yes!"

Jayme smiled. "Then perhaps I should introduce you to BattleAxe Grejore."

And if ever I become Brother-Leader, thought Jayme, then Grejore shall definitely need to be replaced. He's far too independent.

"When?" said Axis.

The interview with Grejore went well. Axis, always sensitive about his scandalous bastardry, had been concerned that the BattleAxe might refuse him on that count alone, but Grejore had not once alluded to it. He questioned Axis at length about his training, and appeared impressed that Axis had studied so many years with Ganelon, whose skill Grejore respected greatly. Then, the interview concluded, Grejore took Axis onto the practice field where, together with eight or nine other Axe-Wielders, he watched Axis demonstrate his skill with weapons.

Axis' partner on the practice field was an Axe-Wielder of about twenty-three or four, tall and fair with friendly hazel eyes, well advanced within the ranks of the Axe-Wielders, and sturdy and skilful with both axe and sword. His name was Belial, and as he took Axis through his paces with first the sword and then the axe, he occasionally nodded, giving Axis a word or two of encouragement, even of praise.

When they had finally stopped, both men sweating, Belial slid his axe back into his weapons' belt and looked over to Grejore.

"He is good, BattleAxe," Belial said, and Axis visibly relaxed, to the point of almost smiling. He is good. Belial had been the toughest opponent Axis had ever faced, better even than Ganelon, and Axis felt enormous relief at Belial's brusque approval.

Grejore walked slowly out onto the practice field, his sharp eyes never once leaving Axis. "But does he have the feel for the axe?" he said, very soft.

For a moment there was silence, then the BattleAxe shifted his glance to Belial. "Well," said Grejore, "there is but one way to find out, isn't there?"

Axis tensed.

Grejore looked back to Axis. "I am willing that you try for the Axe-Wielders, boy, but it is not my decision. You understand that, yes?"

Axis nodded. "The Axe-Wielders serve the Seneschal, and the Seneschal serve Artor. Ultimately the Axe-Wielders serve Artor. Whether or not I join will be His decision."

"And yet you do not look afraid," said Grejore. "Fascinating. Well," he looked back to Belial, "Axis will need an axe-brother. Will you serve?"

Axis almost stopped breathing. He knew a little of the ordeal that all prospective Axe-Wielders endured before they could be admitted into the ranks of the elite force, and one of the things he did know was that the candidate needed an axe-brother to guide him through the test. An axe-brother took personal and total responsibility for a new recruit, and Axis understood that if he failed, then so also would Belial. Their futures in the Axe-Wielders would be entwined. They would rise and fall on each other's strengths and weaknesses.

But more importantly and far more immediately, if Axis failed this ordeal, then Belial would be cast out from the Axe-Wielders (assuming, of course, that both Axis and Belial survived the ordeal). Axis' failure would be Belial's failure. Belial had every right to refuse to act as axe-brother—if he did refuse it would never be held against him—and Axis had heard tales of candidates who spent years trying to find an Axe-Wielder willing to act as axe-brother. What would Belial say? Would he—

"Yes," said Belial. "I will act as axe-brother."

Grejore raised an eyebrow. "Such a quick response, Belial, and so positive. No hesitation. Yet you have refused on the three other occasions I have asked it of you. What is different about this youth?"

Belial looked steadily at Axis as he replied. "When I was a very small boy," he said, "my father took me to court at Carlon. I was scared, for all seemed very frightening, but a lovely woman took me into her care, and spent time with me, and showed me about the palace as if I were her honoured guest." Belial paused, and gave a strange, funny little smile. "I swore her total allegiance. I swore that if ever I could serve her I would." Again he paused. "I never had the chance to serve her as I vowed, but I will not hesitate before her son. It would be my honour to serve as the axe-brother of Princess Rivkah's son."

Axis was dumb-founded. His mother's name was never mentioned before him, let alone spoken with such honour. He wanted to thank Belial, but the words stuck in his throat, and all he could do was stare at the man.

"Very well then," said Grejore. "Tomorrow morning. Savour what hours you have left."

And with that he was gone.

Three hours after sunrise the following morning, Axis stood with Belial before the Tower of the Seneschal.

The entire corps of grey-uniformed Axe-Wielders encircled them, their axes hanging from their weapons'-belts and glinting in the morning sun.

Axis wondered at the trials each and every one of them had gone through.

He must succeed, he must!

What other life could there be for him, save among the Axe-Wielders in service to the Seneschal and the great god Artor?

Hoare, the Brother-Leader of the Seneschal, was present as well, together with Jayme and Moryson and most of the brothers resident within the Tower of the Seneschal. The ordeal of the axe was a significant event, and one witnessed by all those who served, or were served by, the axe.

"There is a new man stands among us," said Hoare, and Axis swallowed, knowing the ordeal had begun. "Who might he be?"

"He is a stranger who seeks admission to our ranks," said Grejore, and Axis felt a further shiver of apprehension as he heard the flatness in the BattleAxe's voice. "We are here to witness whether or not he has the courage and the ability to serve to protect the Seneschal. Our comrade Belial has agreed to stand with him as axe-brother."

Grejore's gaze now shifted to Axis. "Are you willing, boy? Are you willing to meet your axe?"

Are you willing to die?

Axis clenched his fist and tapped it over his heart, bowing first to Hoare and then to Grejore. "I am willing to offer myself to the service of Artor and of the Seneschal who serve Him. I am willing to die, if that is what Artor and my Brother-Leader require."

To one side, unnoticed, Moryson's mouth quirked.

"And if Artor graces me enough that I live through this day," Axis continued, now standing straight and looking Grejore directly in the eye, "then I shall be your axe, to wield as you wish."

"Well, whatever his skill with the axe, at least he's mastered the finer arts of pretty speaking," Hoare muttered. He stepped back to what he thought was a safe distance and waved a hand at Grejore. "Carry on."

Grejore moved close to Belial and Axis, speaking to them quietly but intensely. "You know what this ordeal entails. Are you sure? Both of you?"

"Aye," said the two younger men, as one. Axis gave Belial a grateful look. Belial was trusting Axis with his life, and Axis would give his not to let him down.

Grejore turned to Axis. "Remember," he said, "listen to the song of the axe. Listen to it hum. The axe never lies."

Axis gave a terse nod to acknowledge Grejore's advice, but his eyes had never left Belial's.

Trust the axe, or trust Belial? Which? Intuitively, Axis knew he faced a decision in the next few minutes. Making the wrong one would cost both him and Belial their lives.

Grejore stepped away, leaving Axis and Belial alone within the circle of watches. Belial took a deep breath, and Axis suddenly realised the man was nervous.

"I will not fail you," Axis said, low but fierce.

Belial reached out a hand, resting it on Axis' shoulder. "I know," he said. "Axis, listen to me. In a few short moments Artor will grant you your axe. It is your ordeal whether you allow it to kill you—" and me "—or if you best the axe and take it as your own. Axis, I must blindfold you for this test. You will not be able to see from which direction Artor sends the axe. But I can see, and you must listen to me, and trust me. Both our lives depend on it. Listen to my voice, let it guide you. Trust me, and the axe will be yours."

And both of us will live.

Axis frowned. Belial told him to trust him and to listen to him. That made sense. Belial was his axe-brother, and they needed to bond so that, when it came to desperate battle, they each knew they could rely completely on the other.

But what Grejore had said also made sense. Listen to the song of the axe. Listen to it hum. The axe never lies. He needed to be able to trust the axe, for during his life as an Axe-Wielder, then his axe often would be the only thing to stand between life and death.

What should he do? Listen to Belial, or to the axe?

Belial's hand tightening fractionally on Axis' shoulder. "Axis? Are you ready . . . or do you wish to walk away?"

"I am ready to face Artor's axe," Axis said, and felt rightness sweep through him with that statement.

But which would be righter? Belial's voice, or the song of the axe as it swept towards him?

Belial drew a band of black cloth from a pocket, and bound it about Axis' eyes.

"Trust me," Belial whispered, then he took a step back, visibly steeled himself, and said, "We are ready, Brother-Leader."

Hoare cleared his throat, and raised his hand before him. "Artor! A young man stands before you who begs admission into your service among the Axe-Wielders. I beg you, try him with the power of your axe, that we might know the manner of your will. Is he worthy, or is he not?"

Everyone tensed, brothers of the Seneschal and Axe-Wielders alike. Eyes shifted nervously, muscles jerked as the wind shifted first this way and then that, hands clenched and then unclenched at the sound of the lake lapping against the shore.

No one knew how Artor would deliver the axe.

Belial and Axis stood facing each other, alone in the cleared space before the Tower of the Seneschal. Axis, blindfolded, stood tense and ready, arms slightly bent at his side, ready for that single move only Belial could direct.

Belial, like everyone else, was looking about.

From where would the axe come?

High above, riding his wild plough across the sky, Artor looked down, and beheld the supplicant who wished to join His Axe-Wielders.

Artor looked down, and did not like what He saw.

Belial jerked his eyes upward. High in the sky, glinting out of the sun, a silver axe tumbled slowly out of the sky.

"I see it," he said.

I hear it sing, Axis thought, I hear it sing! Then, directly on the back of that thought, came another: I hear it sing, and it sings wrong.

He felt suddenly very, very afraid. It sings wrong.

"Listen to me, Axis," said Belial, his voice tight, "the axe tumbles down from on high, as if it were an attacking black-winged eagle. Do you understand what I'm saying?"

Yes, Axis understood. Belial was giving him the weight and angle of the axe's fall. It fell as a black-winged eagle attacked—it flies through the air twisting in an unpredictable spiral, as the eagle confuses and disorientates its prey.

"Have you seen how the black-winged eagle concludes its hunt, Axis?"

"Yes." Although the spiral of the eagle's attack appeared unpredictable, it always concluded its attack in the same manner: abruptly swerving out of its spiral to sweep up behind its prey, slamming into the nape of its neck. Belial was telling him that was where the axe was falling . . . towards the nape of his neck. Belial could have told Axis that in words, but he was doing the better thing, giving Axis both visual and instinctive understanding of the nature of the axe's approach.

Yet that was not what the axe sung to Axis. It sung that it fell straight and true as an arrow, and that all he would need do was extend his right hand, and the handle of the axe would slap into it.

"Trust me, Axis," Belial whispered.

Trust me, whispered the axe.

Axis was now so tense, so confused, he could barely keep still. He could feel the weight of the regard of all who stood and witnessed.

He could feel the axe hurtling towards him!

Who to trust, Belial . . . or the axe?

Artor, if he chose wrong then he would murder any chance that he had of escaping the stain of his birth! He would murder any chance he had of living . . .

He could feel the axe hurtling . . .

All Axis wanted to do was to sink into a defensive crouch and tear the blindfold away from his eyes. And if he could not do that, then all he wanted to do was listen to the song of the axe . . . oh, how he wanted to listen to the song of the axe as it danced through the air!

He could feel the axe . . .

"Trust me," Belial whispered again.

Artor! He could feel the axe whisper through the air, feel the cold edge of its wicked blade as it hurtled towards him. All he needed to do was to put out his right hand . . . now . . . NOW! . . . and the axe would be his, if only he put out his right hand and—

"Now!" Belial shouted, and although Axis had been visualising thrusting out his right hand to feel the axe smack home true—he had seen it, he had felt it, he knew it was the right thing to do!—instead he ducked and twisted to his left, throwing his hands up, then gasping in shock as he felt the weight and coldness of the axe's handle slam into his palms.

The force of the axe's impact almost pushed him over, but Axis managed to regain his balance. He stood, hefting the god-gifted axe easily in his right hand as with his left he tore the blindfold from his eyes.

The Axe-Wielders were roaring, hands pumping into the sky, but for the moment Axis had eyes for no one but Belial.

The axe had sung wrong, but Belial had spoken truly.

"The allegiance I once swore to your mother is now yours, Axis," Belial said softly. "Welcome to the Axe-Wielders."

Axis saw the relief in the man's eyes. If Axis had not ducked and twisted and caught the axe as it flew towards the nape of his neck, then the blade would have taken off Axis' head the instant before it would have taken Belial's.

It was a lesson Axis never forgot, through all the trials of his life.

Trust Belial before the axe.

Far above, Artor raged as he drove His plough across the sky.

That axe had been meant to murder.

HOW THE ICARII FOUND THEIR WINGS

As Orr partly explained to Azhure in *BattleAxe*, the Icarii, as
the Charonites and the human race of Tencendor, the Acharites,
were all born of the ancient Enchantress. She had three sons,
fathered by the gods only alone knew, and of those three sons
she favoured only the younger two. To them she whispered some
of her myriad secrets, while the eldest she cast from her door and
turned her back on his pleas. This eldest wandered desolate into
the land, which he eventually desolated to assuage his grief at
his mother's rejection, while his younger brothers stayed many
more years at the Enchantress' knee . . . learning . . . learning . . .
learning . . .

"You have a duty," she told her middle son, "to wander and
watch." He nodded, and thought he understood.

"You have a duty," she told her youngest son, "to dance your
delight to the stars." And he too nodded, thinking he understood.

When the Enchantress died, her hair silvered but her face
untouched by weariness, her two younger made their way into the
world. The middle brother was reflective, and haunted shadows,

thinking there to catch a glimpse of the unknowable. Eventually his eyes turned downwards to the chasms that led into the earth, and there he eventually made his way.

The youngest brother was wide of smile and bright of curiosity. He clutched in his hand his mother's ring, that which would give birth to all of the Enchanter's rings and which would eventually find its way home to Azhure's hand, and it impelled him to cast his eye to the high places, and there he eventually climbed.

All three brothers proliferated. They took to themselves many wives from among the humanoid races that populated the land, and these wives bore them many children. These children took to themselves husbands and wives, and they likewise bred many children. Within a thousand years the plains and the chasms and the mountains rang with the voices of the brother races: Mankind, the Acharites, who followed their cattle through dusty plain trails and built themselves houses of brick; the Charonites, who explored the misty waterways beneath the trails and took the houses others had left behind; and the Icarii, beloved of the gods, who climbed the crags and cried out to the stars and built themselves houses of music and mystery.

Then, the Icarii did not have wings.

The story of how the Icarii found their wings is rightly the love story of EverHeart and CrimsonStar. CrimsonStar was an Enchanter unparalled in the history of the Icarii, but his love for the stars and for the Star Dance paled into insignificance beside the love he bore his wife, EverHeart. CrimsonStar and EverHeart lived in the lower ranges of the Icescarp Alps. Then, so long before the Wars of the Axe, the Icarii populated most of the mountain ranges of Tencendor, most living in the Minaret Peaks (those peaks the Acharites would later call the Bracken Ranges). But CrimsonStar and EverHeart were newly married and preferred to enjoy the relative isolation of the Icescarp Alps. Talon Spike was only just being opened up and hollowed out, and the few dozen Icarii within their immediate vicinity were, truth to tell, a few dozen too many for CrimsonStar and EverHeart.

They did what they could to keep themselves distant, climbing frightening precipes to achieve privacy to indulge their frequent cravings for love, clinging to razorbacked crags to evade curious eyes and to allow the winds of thrill and danger to deepen their passion.

They were in love and they were young, and so they were indulged by their elders. Time enough, in fifty years or so, for them to descend from the heights of newly-married explorations.

But fifty years they did not have. Eight years after they were married, when they had barely recovered from the breathless passion of their initial consummation, EverHeart fell.

She fell from a peak so high even the winds were frightened to assail it. She fell so far she was swallowed by the clouds that broiled about the knees of the mountain.

She fell so fast even CrimsonStar's scream could not follow her.

It took him three days to find her, and when he did, he thought he had found a corpse. She lay broken, unmoving, her spilt blood frozen in crazy patterns across the rocks that cradled her. CrimsonStar's tears felt as if they, too, were freezing into solid grief as they trailed down his cheeks. He touched his wife, but she did not move, and her flesh had the solidness of rock.

Frozen.

He wailed, then screamed, then wrenched his wife from her resting place, tearing her skin where it had frozen to the surface of the rocks. He cuddled her close, trying to warm her, then realised through his grief that somewhere deep within EverHeart, her courageous heart, her ever heart, still thudded. Slowly, achingly slowly, but still it thudded.

He carried her back to their home, and there he cared for her, bringing to her side all the Healers of the Icarii people, and even calling to her side Banes from the distant forests. They restored her warmth, and the colour to her cheeks. They restored the brightness of her eye, and even the gloss of her golden hair. They restored the flex to her arms and the suppleness to her long white fingers.

But they could not restore movement or usefulness to her shattered legs, and they could not restore the laughter to her face.

Everheart was condemned to lie useless in her bed, her lower body anchoring her to immobility, its flesh a drain on the resources of her upper body and, more importantly, on her spirit.

At CrimsonStar's request, the Icarii Healers and the Avar Banes left. They farewelled the pair as best they could, certain that EverHeart would not survive the year, and even more certain CrimsonStar would not survive his wife's inevitable death.

For seven months CrimsonStar held EverHeart's hand, and sang to her, and soothed her as best he could. He fed her and washed her and ministered to her needs. He lived only to see her smile, and to hear her tell him she was content.

But EverHeart could do neither of these things without lying, and this she would not do.

One night, late into the darkness, EverHeart asked CrimsonStar to kill her. It was a brutal request, but EverHeart was too tired of life to phrase it more politely.

"I cannot," CrimsonStar said, and turned his head aside.

"Then build me wings to fly," Everheart said, bitterness twisting her voice, "that I may escape these useless legs and this prison-bed."

CrimsonStar looked at her. "My lovely, I cannot . . . "

"Then kill me."

CrimsonStar crept away, not wishing EverHeart to see the depth of his distress. Knowing she knew it anyway.

He climbed to the crag from which EverHeart had fallen so many months before. He had no intention of throwing himself from the peak, but some instinct told him that he might find comfort at the same point where he and she had lost so much of their lives. He sat down in a sheltered crevice, and watched the stars filter their way across the night sky.

Tears ran down his face. Everheart had given him an impossible request . . . and if he didn't help her die now, then what agony of wasting would she go through over the next few months until she died of unaided causes?

"You should not weep so at this altitude," a soft voice said, "for your tears will freeze to your face and leaved your cheeks marred with black ice."

CrimsonStar jerked his head up.

A sparrow hopped into the crevice, its feathers ruffled out against the cold.

CrimsonStar was so stunned he could not speak.

"I have been disappointed in you, my son," the sparrow continued, and hopped onto CrimsonStar's knee so he could the better look the Icarii man in the eye.

"Disappointed?" CrimsonStar managed, but he straightened his shoulders and brushed the tears from his eyes. Who was this sparrow to so chastise him?

"I am your father, CrimsonStar."

"No . . . no . . . my father is FellowStar . . . alive and well . . . "

The sparrow tipped its head to one side, its eyes angry yet sadly tolerant of his wayward child. "Do you not understand, CrimsonStar? I am the father of the Icarii race."

CrimsonStar could do nothing but stare at the sparrow.

"I lay with the Enchantress, and she waxed great with our child. Her third and last son for her life . . . and my fourth son that spring. It was a good spring for me that year."

"I . . . I did not know . . . "

"Few knew who the Enchantress took to her bed, child. The fathers of her elder sons are unknown to me. And I . . . I should not have told you of my role in your generation, save that I could not bear your sadness and that of EverHeart's. Still," the sparrow sighed, "I had no choice, for you have proved such a disappointment, and all fathers reserve their right to chastise and redirect their children."

CrimsonStar slowly shook his head from side to side, almost unable to comprehend that this sparrow (a *sparrow*!) was the father of the proud Icarii race.

"Listen to me, CrimsonStar. I shall tell you of a great joy and then I shall curse you, because you must pay for the privilege of hearing my advice—"

"No . . . I have been cursed enough."

"You have no choice, my son. Now . . . watch."

And the sparrow fluttered his wings, and rose a handspan above CrimsonStar's knee before settling gently down again. "Why have you no wings, CrimsonStar?"

"Wings . . . ?"

"Wings, CrimsonStar. You are my son, and yet you refuse to wear your heritage."

"I . . ."

"Do you not sing the Flight Song to your children as they lie nesting in their shells?"

"Flight Song . . . ?"

The sparrow spat in disgust. "Listen." And he trilled a simple song, paused, then trilled it again. "Repeat it."

His suprise giving way to a small thrill of excitement, CrimsonStar repeated the tune, stumbling over one or two of the phrases, but correcting himself instantly.

The sparrow laughed. "You *are* my son, CrimsonStar! Now go home and lay beside EverHeart and sing her the Song. Run your hands down her back, rub, probe, encourage, and soon she shall have movement again. Soon she will soar free from her prison-bed and let the sky ring with her laughter. Teach her the Song, and let her minister to you as well. And when she swells with your child, then place your hands on her belly and sing to the child what I have taught you. It is my gift to my children, CrimsonStar."

"Thank—"

"Do not thank me, CrimsonStar. Not until after the pain has faded, for you are both late in age to spread your wings. Besides, for the knowledge I have imparted and the gift I have given I must curse you."

CrimsonStar waited, sure the curse would match the gift.

"Oh, it will, it will, CrimsonStar. Listen to me now. You and Everheart will be the first among the Icarii to spread your wings and fly into the heavens. But for this there is a price. I name your family SunSoar, a regal name, for your feathered backs must bear the burden of the sins of the Icarii. Wait . . . there is more. As you and EverHeart can consider no other love save that you bear for the other, so no SunSoar will love beyond the SunSoar blood. Never will you and yours find happiness save in each other's arms. Do you understand?"

CrimsonStar nodded soberly, considering the implications.

"Then go down to your wife, CrimsonStar. And then to your people . . . and tell them the heavens wait."

AUTHOR'S NOTE

One of my editors came across this story online and asked that it be incorporated into one of my books. I know I used it somewhere within the Wayfarer Redemption trilogy, but can't remember the book it is in!

THE COROLEANS

The Corolean Empire is massive, approximately three times the size of Tencendor. Attached to Tencendor only by a small isthmus, the Corolean Empire stretches south for almost a thousand leagues, and east-west in a great bulge, sixteen hundred leagues at its widest point. Because it is so vast, the land varies from the great dry Haki Desert (occupying the western central portion of the land) to the frigid eastern Jai Alps that spear uninhabitable barren rock into the sky. Despite the extremes of alp and desert, the majority of the Empire is warm and humid and utterly flat. There are numerous rivers, plentiful swamps complete with swarms of noxious insects, and vast gloamy black plains that the Corolean slaves till to produce grain and fruits (only slaves till the gloamy plains because of the inevitability of footrot and ankle gangrene in the damp and warm soils). In the low hills surrounding the black plains farmers, barely free themselves, raise herds of goats and pigs (the main meat supply), keep a few thin cows for milk, and wonder if they shouldn't diversify into dates and sun-baked bricks to avoid falling into debt and the ignominies of slavery.

Corolean society is similar to, and yet different from, Tencendorian society. There is a single humanoid race (although rumours circulate about a race of shy swamp men) dominated by the noble caste. The Corolean nobility is of ancient lineage—and the bloodlines of the Forty-Four-Hundred First Families are kept rigorously free of any contamination from the lower castes. The Forty-Four-Hundred marry only among themselves, and they admit no new blood, no matter how wealthy some upstart trader has made himself on date-milk supply. They live in vast palace complexes on the airy ranges overlooking the major towns and cities of Coroleas, and spend the worst of the humid season in the cool foothills of the Jai Alps. They control all political and social power, appoint the High Priests from among themselves, and own the vast majority of the land. No one can own an armed band or a shipping vessel unless he be of the Forty-Four-Hundred.

Every ten years the male heads of each family gather to elect a new Emperor from among their own. This election process is complex and tiring—the Forty-Four-Hundred Heads remain in seclusion for months until it is completed, and not a few perish during this time from old age, poison, jewelled daggers in the gut, and from hopeless attempts to expend pent-up sexual energies at the boardgame of Fillip. Once a new Emperor is elected there is great relief, and some sadness at finding the old Emperor unexplainably dead in a bed tangled with blood-stained sheets. The new Emperor orders all games of contaminated and/or desecrated Fillip burned, and the Forty-Four-Hundred Heads are released from their incarceration.

The Thirty-Eight-Thousand Second Families are wealthy, educated and too intelligent for their own good, yet they share in none of the political, social and religious power of the Forty-Four-Hundred. Most of the Thirty-Eight-Thousand have made their fortunes at trade, either with Tencendor, or with the lands across the Widowmaker Sea. Some are slave traders of great wit, skill and deception. Despite their wealth, intelligence and lust for some say in how Coroleas is governed, the Thirty-Eight-Thousand wield almost no power. They are not allowed to own land unless the sale be approved by a committee of forty-four Heads from the Forty-Four-Hundred. None among the Thirty-Eight-Thousand Second Families can wear silk or fur, nor cloth of any weave that is dyed scarlet, ivory or gold, and they may not own or wear pearls or rubies. They may not play Fillip.

They may, however, man the bureaucracy, and the larger portion of Corolean administration is run by powerful men from the Thirty-Eight-Thousand who have grown bored with trade. Members of the Thirty-Eight-Thousand also provide the larger number of diplomats (although not ambassadors who come from the Forty-Four-Hundred) and officers in the large, potent and numerous Corolean armies (most of the Forty-Four-Hundred own at least one army). Most of the professions and the scholarly academies are manned by members of the Thirty-Eight-Thousand. Their daughters, if fortunate, may be chosen at the annual Rivermud Festival to become the toy of a Forty-Four-Hundred man for the space of a year (or however long she lives . . . whichever ends first). Whenever there is an internal rebellion (and there are at least four or five of them each year), it is usually funded, if not led, by one of the Thirty-Eight-Thousand families intent on somehow toppling the Forty-Four-Hundred from their pinnacle of power. In twelve hundred years of trying the Thirty-Eight-Thousand have come no closer to penetrating the society of the Forty-Four-Hundred than they have come to purchasing a single board game of Fillip. They spend many nights talking of emigrating, but are too aware of their own privileges to actually do anything about it.

The Third is the general name given to the mass of men, women and children who work to serve the Forty-Four-Hundred and the Thirty-Eight-Thousand but who are not quite (not quite yet) slaves. They rent farming land for rates often beyond their means, run the river and sea boats (if not own them), man the markets, build and repair the homes of the upper castes, lay and dig the roads and the canals, slaughter—then skin and gut—the goats and pigs, fish the rivers, mow the lawns, glaze the roof tiles, keep the sewage pipes free of blockages . . . in fact all the heavy and dirty work needed to keep the societies of the two upper Corolean castes merry and greased is done by the Third. The men of the Third provide the foot soldiers for the armies, the rowers for the war boats, and the means to stage grand tournaments and games for the two upper castes. The Third are massively unhappy with their lot, but know not how to improve it beyond staging futile rebellions during the humid and oppressive nights of the wet season. When not rebelling, they find release in breeding.

The lot of the slaves is almost beyond despair. They are the men and women who have fallen into such poverty they sell their bodies, wombs and souls to the highest bidder. Their bodies till the gloam plains until they rot and fall apart, their wombs are used by men from the free who need inexpensive bastards to clean their kitchens and stables, their souls are toyed with by the rich until their amusement dies along with the slave. And yet the lot of the slaves is revered by the Forty-Four-Hundred and the Thirty-Eight-Thousand who argue that a life of slavery is one to be envied for its freedom from political and financial duplicities. Nobles and scholars applaud the grind of slavery for its inherent nobleness ... and yet how few of the Forty-Four-Hundred or the Thirty-Eight-Thousand know the feel of the black soil eating for month after month at the skin of ankle and shin, or can comprehend the pain endured in breeding a bastard for the stables, or understand the screaming nightmares as High Priests finger the souls of those picked to pleasure the wealthy. Slaves live to die, and no-one knows that better than the slaves themselves.

Such is their despair they think not of revolt, but only of the release of the final obliteration.

The Forty-Four-Hundred, the Thirty-Eight-Thousand and the Third revere a multitude of bronze deities. Among the Third are a caste of bronze workers, strictly controlled by the bronze merchant guild of the Thirty-Eight-Thousand, who make small bronze figurines that form the outer shell of the god. These figurines can be worn about the body (generally hanging from a belt, but the very religious sometimes insert them into bodily cavities) or stood on shelves within the home. But the figurines are useless until they are given power. Each figurine is empowered by the soul of a man or women. Slaves provide the soul. Once a figurine is finished and purchased, then the buyer must also purchase a soul to inhabit the figurine and give it power. The younger the soul, the better. Newborn babies who have not yet taken suck are best of all, but so prohibitively expensive they can only be purchased by members of the Forty-Four-Hundred. When the life has been obtained, then the soul must be released from the body. This is generally done in as long a religious ceremony as possible, presided over by as high a Priest as possible, and with the most possible enjoyment by the onlookers. A Priest must be skilled enough to draw the soul from the living body it currently lives in with the greatest possible pain, for this gives the soul—and thus the bronze deity it is placed into—the greatest possible power. The soul can live in a bronze figurine for many centuries before its potency fades and it is cast out as scrap metal to be melted down and re-soulled.

Few foreigners understand or sympathise with the Corolean obsession with bronze deities and stolen souls, but the Coroleans care little for what outsiders think of them. What other use the soul of a slave, anyway?

THE MISTRESS OF MARWOOD HAGG

THE MISTRESS OF MARWOOD HAGG

JANUARY 1583, COUNTY DURHAM, ENGLAND

Edmund Lewkenor, Earl of Henley, stood at the edge of the battlefield and surveyed his victory. The rain that had blighted the entire day continued to sleet across the grey landscape, and Henley winced at its sudden icy touch across his sweaty face as his squire removed his helm. Henley gestured impatiently, and the squire hastened to unbuckle the heaviest pieces of armoured plate from about his lord's body, then handed Henley a thick worsted cloak.

Lionel Fitzherbert, one of Henley's senior commanders, materialised out of the driving rain, hunching inside his own cloak. Its lower folds clung about his legs, the material sodden with mud thrown up by the rain.

"Where is he?" Henley said.

Fitzherbert's head jerked towards a depression in the field. "Over there, my lord." He tugged once or twice at his muddied, water-logged cloak, then let his hand fall. There would be no warmth to be found this terrible day.

Henley shot his commander sharp look. "Alive?"

Fitzherbert shrugged, too exhausted to find the words for a reply after a vicious battle that had raged for over ten hours.

Henley grunted, looking towards the depression that Fitzherbert had indicated. He hoped the bastard Earl of Chelmsford *was* still alive, for he deserved the full pitilessness of Queen Elizabeth's justice for his unholy rebellion.

Damned Catholics and their Popish plots!

And look to what had their dishonour brought them—the most contemptuous of deaths in this luckless, bemired landscape. Chelmsford had picked a gently undulating and recently ploughed field for his battle with the Queen's army, and God Himself had sent his judgement in the form of this rain, turning the soft, giving earth into a clinging black deadly quagmire. Now the field was marred with the dark featureless clumps of corpses settling deeper into the ooze: hundreds, if not thousands, of rebels now manured the sodden earth with their rotting hopes and ambitions. Worse, many of Henley's own soldiers lay mired side by side with their foes, both rebels and defenders made brothers in the cold ooze of their shared muddied death.

"Let's not waste time," Henley said, and together the two men, accompanied by a contingent of men-at-arms, squelched their way towards the central depression of the battlefield.

It was a slow, difficult journey. With every step Henley and his companions sank over their ankles into the battle-churned slime. If Henley had thought the horses would prove faster, he would have ridden, but as it was this field would have eaten the weighty destriers up to their bellies.

As they approached the depression, disfigured with the fallen, mud-covered bodies of foot soldiers and knights alike, Henley saw that several of his men were attempting to lift one of the fallen knights from the field.

Chelmsford? Henley wondered, and hurried as much as he could.

As he reached the struggling group, treading over several corpses as the easiest and most efficient means of covering the final few paces, Henley realised that the fallen man was, indeed, accoutred in Chelmsford's heraldic devices.

"Sweet Lord Christ," Henley muttered as he drew level with the four of his men trying to raise the rebel from the muddied field, "save him to face our Queen's justice!"

And with that mutter, his men slipped, and Chelmsford fell from their grasp, his heavily armoured body sinking back into the mud.

The rebel baron struggled, his arms waving, his mailed hands outreaching for aid, his helmeted head writhing within the cold embrace of the rain-soaked earth.

A sound issued from within his helmet—a frightful, desperate combination of gasp and gurgle.

"Get his helmet off!" Henley snapped, and two of his men pulled off their leather gloves, and, risking their own stability, leaned forward and unbuckled Chelmsford's heavy helm.

It moved, but not enough, and their efforts perversely pushed Chelmsford's armour-weighted head deeper into the mud.

"For the Lord's sake!" Henley said. "Get it off—*now!*"

The two men put in a final effort, and with a grudging squelch the helmet at last surrendered. The men staggered back, and the helmet fell into the mud to one side of Chelmsford's head.

Henley drew in a sharp breath, shocked by what he saw. Chelmsford's head was all but submerged in the liquefied soil— it covered his forehead, cheeks and chin and lapped at his mouth.

Chelmsford's eyes, however, were incongruously free of the mud, and they stared at Henley, pale blue, bulging, frantic. The rebel baron open his mouth, meaning to add words to the plea in his eyes, but as he did so the mud surged and rose up about him, sliding into his nostrils and pouring into the void between his lips, and the only plea that issued from Chelmsford's mouth was a great bubble of air that burst with the stink of escaping marsh gas.

Henley's men leaned down again, horror hastening their hands, but Henley stopped them with quick gesture.

"Leave him," he said. "*This* is justice, no better."

Chelmsford's eyes, impossibly, widened even further, their pale blue turning to pink as terror burst a score of blood vessels within their orbs.

He struggled, frantic, and the mud gurgled and bubbled in his mouth and flooded his nostrils and the air passages of his sinuses.

"Cursed rebel," Henley muttered. "Accept your fate without grudging." He paused, then placed one of his feet in the centre of Chelmsford's armour-plated chest and bore down with all his weight.

Chelmsford had died in his own county, a mere two days' journey from his home base of Castle Marwood Hagg, and it was to Marwood Hagg that the Earl of Henley—together with an armed escort of several thousand men—escorted his body.

It was, after all, to Henley's advantage to ensure that Chelmsford's widow did not harbour rebellious ambitions of her own, or shelter supporters of her lately deceased husband. A viewing of what happened to those who *did* think to challenge Queen Elizabeth's right to rule over the largely Catholic north of England would undoubtedly do these papists the world of good.

They approached Marwood Hagg as a cold dusk gathered. Crows circled through the low clouds, and soared about the crenellated towers of the castle. Silent, sullen peasants stood in huddled groups at the edges of their stubbled fields, watching expressionless as the bier carrying their lord's corpse trundled past.

Sentinels of death, Henley thought, and did not know if he meant the crows with that thought, or the silent, watching peasants.

The castle stood open to them, its gates rolled back, its sentries absent from its parapets.

A single figure stood in the open gateway, and Henley signalled his escort to a halt as he rode forward alone.

"My lady," Henley said, reining his horse to a stop before her.

Eleanor, Countess of Chelmsford and mistress of Marwood Hagg, was a young woman, full twenty-five years her husband's junior. Despite her relative youth, there seemed a quality of weariness about her thin, tall frame, as if she had lived a little too desperately during her thirty-odd years.

She was veiled in grey and robed in scarlet, and beneath her veil her face was pale and lined, as if she had spent long hours in tearless grief. There was no fear nor respect in her brief regard of Henley, but when her gaze settled on the bier at the fore of the escort her composure momentarily deserted her. She took a sharp breath, her cheeks blotching with colour. "You have brought home my husband?"

"Aye, my lady."

Eleanor inclined her head towards Henley, in control once more. "Then I thank you, my lord."

And with that she turned and walked into the courtyard.

Henley watched her narrow, straight figure for a moment, then kicked his horse forward, waving to his escort to follow.

They carried the Earl of Chelmsford's corpse to the chapel and it was to this chapel that Henley took himself after he had rested and eaten.

The countess had instructed that her husband's corpse be laid upon the altar and now, as Henley approached, she stood behind it straight and still, her hands clasped lightly before her, the veil folded back from her impassive face.

Henley scarcely noticed her, so appalled was he at the state of Chelmsford's corpse. Instead of being suitably robed and draped, the countess had caused her husband's remains to be stripped. Now the Earl of Chelmsford's white body lay naked atop the altar, his arms hanging towards the floor, his massive belly mounding towards the stone-vaulted roof, his face, hands and genitals mottling and bloating in the first stages of putrefaction.

Henley slowly raised his gaze to the countess. "My lady? Why have you not attired your husband decently and with respect?"

"Because I am mystified, my lord."

"Mystified?"

Eleanor swept one graceful hand down the length of her husband's body. "My beloved husband has died in battle, yet I see not a single wound upon him. How was his death accomplished, my lord, if not through means of foul witchcraft?"

Henley's neck reddened, the only sign of his discomposure. "There has been no witchcraft or foulness in the manner of your husband's death, my lady, save in that he brought his death upon himself in his most vile rebellion against our good Queen Elizabeth."

"*Your* good Queen Elizabeth," Eleanor said softly, "for we do not honour her in these northern counties." Her voice strengthened. "I ask again, how is it that there is no wound on my husband's body? In what manner did he die?"

Henley remembered that instant his men had pulled Chelmsford's helm from his head, remembered Chelmsford's frantic pale eyes staring at Henley from amid their sea of mud, remembered their silent scream for aid.

And, in remembering, Henley felt no regret for his lack of mercy towards the terrified, dying man.

"He died," he said, his tone icy, "when he fell from his horse into the thick mud of the battlefield. His weighty armour dragged him down, and he drowned, my lady, drowned in the mud as it flowed through his mouth and nostrils and swamped his lungs. Our Lord God vouchsafed unto your husband a death most fitting for his treacherous soul."

Eleanor's entire body stiffened, as if she fought for control. In this effort she was partly unsuccessful, for when she spoke, her voice trembled very slightly. "And in his muddied drowning, my lord, did any attempt to aid him?"

"It *was* a death most fitting, my lady," Henley said, "and I had no thought to interrupt it."

There was a moment of utter, cold silence in the chapel, then the Earl of Henley turned his back and strode away.

Behind him, the mistress of Marwood Hagg sagged in horror, and she leaned her hands on the altar so she would not entirely sink to the stone floor.

"My dear sweet lord," she whispered, bending her face close to that of her dead husband's, "they murdered you with *mud?*"

Then Eleanor looked down the chapel to where Henley had disappeared, and both her face and her voice strengthened. "Then will mud dog your murderer's every footstep, my lord. Mud shall consume his hopes, as it has consumed mine."

She buried her husband the next morning. The Earl of Henley attended, for he would not ride out for his home in Suffolk until noon.

By which time, he prayed to God, this dismal weather would have turned into something more conducive to journeying.

Besides, Henley meant to ensure that Chelmsford had a proper Church of England service said over his rotting, treacherous bastard of a corpse. There would be no papist heresy muttered here.

The small graveyard attached to the village church stood a half mile from Marwood Hagg. Like most graveyards, it faced east, so that the morning sun could chase away evil shadows and sprites from the sleeping dead.

But there would be little chance of sun this morning, Henley thought, hunching closer inside his cloak. Heavy rain clouds rumbled across the sky, swollen and misshapen as if demons cavorted within their midst, and a hard, biting wind blew down from the north. It made Henley wonder if such foul weather normally attended upon Chelmsford; perchance it was merely the reflection of his dark soul.

He shuddered, and to distract himself studied the people attending the service.

There were relatively few.

Eleanor, still dressed in her scarlet robe and grey veil, and apparently unconcerned by her lack of a cloak against the approaching storm. Her entire being was still and silent, and her eyes rested unblinkingly on Henley who stood the other side of the black, open grave.

Two women attended her, as well Chelmsford's estate steward and the seneschal of the castle.

Five peasants, their thick woollen robes twisting in the wind, stood seven or eight paces away, their faces turned towards Henley.

Apart from the priest, and a deacon from a neighbouring parish, the only other people in attendance were six of Henley's men-at-arms. There, not only to protect their lord from any danger, but to man-handle Chelmsford's corpse into his grave.

Back to the mud, where it had died.

The corpse itself lay at the feet of the priest, crosswise to the grave. It was wrapped in a linen shroud, its seams roughly sewn together with twine.

Henley shivered, wishing that Eleanor had chosen to have her husband interred within the church—as would have been fit and proper for a man of his rank. *Why wish to have him interred in the soil, in the open, naked to the elements?*

Finally, impatient and uncomfortable, Henley nodded once at the priest, willing him into action.

The man was nervous, his tongue playing about his lips, his weight shifting from foot to foot.

"Begin," Eleanor said, not moving her regard from Henley.

The priest cleared his throat, and the Book of Common Prayer wobbled in his hands.

Henley wondered how familiar the priest was with it.

"As you wish, my lady," the priest said, his voice high and strained, and, looking down to the prayer book, began the Order for the Burial of the Dead.

He rattled the words out, running them together in a litany of discomfort.

"Speak slowly and clearly," Eleanor said, finally turning her face to the priest, "for otherwise you dishonour my husband!"

The priest halted, swallowed, and then spoke again, his voice now wooden and ponderous in his attempts to please the countess.

"Man that is born of woman hath but a short time to live," he read, "and his life is full of misery—"

Eleanor's eyes snapped back to Henley and her veil lifted away from her face in great gust of wind.

"He cometh up and is cut down like a flower—"

Eleanor bared her teeth at Henley, her face a silent rictus of hate.

Henley was horrified. *What was the woman about?*

"—and he flieth as it were a shadow," the priest continued, trying his best to ignore Eleanor's actions, "and never continueth in one stay. In the midst of life we be in death—"

Eleanor bared her teeth again, then hissed, her face twisting visciously.

"Be still, woman!" Henley said.

Eleanor's face contorted once more, and at her sides her hands clenched into fists.

The priest stumbled into silence, and Henley gestured impatiently to him to continue. *Lord God, all he wanted was to get out of here, and leave this maddened woman to her festering anger!*

Another gust of wind rocked the group standing about the corpse and open grave, and this time it bore on its wings the needle-sting of approaching rain.

"Forasmuch as it hath pleased Almighty God," the priest said, his words once again tumbling over themselves, "of His great mercy to take unto Himself the soul of our dear brother here departed—"

Above them the heavens opened, and the rain sheeted down, drenching everyone within heartbeats.

Eleanor shrieked, making everyone start, then sank to her knees at the graveside.

"Continue!" Henley hissed at the priest, who had closed the Book of Common Prayer and tucked it away under his robes away from the rain.

Eleanor wailed, and tore the veil from her head. Her black hair tumbled over her shoulders, and she lifted her face to the rain, her wails growing ever louder and more pitiful.

"We therefore," the priest said, almost shouting now above the sound of both elements and Eleanor, "commit his body to the ground—"

Eleanor screamed, and her hands grabbed at the neckline of her gown. She ripped it apart, exposing her creamy breasts to both weather and the shocked eyes of the mourners.

The priest tore his gaze away, fixing it on the grave before him. Despite the chill of the rain and wind, his face had flooded with colour. "Earth to earth—"

Eleanor's wails and shrieks rose to an almost unbearable level, and her hands buried themselves in her sodden tresses, tearing out great chunks of hair and flesh from her scalp.

Blood poured over her forehead, diluting in the rain to wash in pink rivulets down her distorted, shrieking face.

"For the Lord's sake!" Henley muttered, and began to move around the grave, intending to slap some sense into the woman.

"Ashes to ashes—"

Eleanor's cries collapsed into a frightful moaning, and her hands tore her robe even further asunder. She smacked at her breasts with open hands, the noise shockingly sharp and hard amid the rumble of the intensifying storm.

The rivulets of blood washed down over her chest, and her beating hands smeared blood all over her breasts.

Henley slipped a little in the muddied earth at the foot of the grave, and he cursed.

Save for Eleanor, Henley and the priest, everyone else had now stepped well back from the grave site, and several had abandoned the service entirely to slip and slide their way through the mud towards the church.

As Henley moved towards her, Eleanor suddenly leaned down to the wet soil, her fingers clutching into the mud.

"And dust to dust," the priest said.

"Dust to dust, *and mud to mud!*" Eleanor cried, lifting her hands and hurling handfuls of the sodden earth into Henley's face. *"Mud to mud!"*

It spatted into his eyes and mouth, and stopped him dead in his tracks.

"Witch!" he yelled, reaching blindly towards her.

"The Lord bless him and keep him," the priest shrieked, and Henley could hear from his voice that he, too, was now dashing towards the church, "and the Lord make His face to shine upon him and be gracious unto him and give him peace!"

Mud to mud, Henley heard Eleanor's now calm voice echoing into his mind. *Mud to mud . . .*

"Amen," Eleanor said softly, as a blinded Henley's right foot slipped at the edge of the grave, and the earl tumbled in, sinking deep into the mud meant for Chelmsford's corpse.

OCTOBER 1583, SUFFOLK

Edmund Lewkenor, Earl of Henley, stood in the great hall of his castle in Suffolk, and thought on how the Lord God had blessed him. These past ten months since his return from disposing of the Earl of Chelmsford and his ill-conceived rebellion had been good to him. Queen Elizabeth, pleased at his quick and successful action against Chelmsford, had heaped preferments upon him; he had arranged advantageous marriages for his two eldest daughters; the harvest on all of his estates had proved spectacular; and tonight . . . tonight his beloved wife Alice lay within her birthing chamber, labouring with the child he had conceived upon her on his return from the north and which, so every astrologer he'd consulted had assured him, was finally his yearned for son and heir.

Henley stood alone by the fire in the massive hearth at the northern end of the hall, sipping a fine spiced ale. Behind the screens at the other end of the hall he could see the occasional movements of the midwives as they hurried between kitchens and the stairs leading up to the birthing chamber, carrying urns of warmed water, vials of herbs, and quantities of linens.

In the far north, the mistress of Marwood Hagg issued forth from her castle. She walked with great purpose, and upon her face was an infinite peace.

She had garbed herself in the same, if mended, scarlet robe she'd worn at her husband's funeral.

The hurried movements of the midwives did not concern Henley. This would be Alice's eighth birth, and her seven previous had all been mercifully sweet and brief (if all ending in the production of yet another daughter). This time, Henley fully expected to greet the dawn with a healthy son and a recovering wife.

Henley took another sip of the spiced ale, his eyes drifting to the great leaded windows in the hall's eastern wall. It was deep autumn now, and the wind threw scatterings of dead leaves against the glass.

The fire warmed Henley's back, and the ale his belly, and he smiled, content with his lot.

She walked directly to the grave of her husband. Strangely, considering the many months that had passed, the earth still lumped fresh and loose atop the grave.

Eleanor noted the condition of the grave with satisfaction, then smiled, love transfiguring her face into an unexpected beauty.

Disregarding the wind that twisted the robe about her body, she knelt down by the fresh-turned earth.

A sudden, harder gust of wind rattled the windows of Henley's hall. The noise was close followed by a thump from the floor above him.

Henley's cup of ale stilled on its way to his mouth, and his eyes cast upwards.

Nothing. Henley relaxed. It was just the wind, and the timber joists creaking in the cold that blew down from the north.

Eleanor lifted her face to the dark sky and tore the veil from her head, allowing her black hair to unravel in the wind.

As her veil fluttered away, the clouds opened in a violent rainstorm.

Rain suddenly squalled viciously against the windows, and Henley jumped, almost dropping his cup of ale.

Frowning, he placed the cup on a nearby table, and looked once more towards the windows.

It was dark now, but he could make out the shadowy waves of the rain beating against the thick glass.

It was almost as if it was angry . . . as if it wanted to gain entry into the peace of Henley's hall—*and of his life*—and drag Henley's contentment . . .

"Down into the mud," Eleanor whispered.

She smiled once again as the rain pelted into the loose earth of her husband's grave, but this time something harder and more deadly than love underlay her expression.

Vengeance was the last service she could do her husband.

Unbidden, memories of the horrifying day of Chelmsford's burial flooded Henley's mind: Eleanor's shrieking and self mutilation; her hurling of the blinding mud into his face; his own tumble into the grave meant for Chelmsford.

It had taken all six of his men-at-arms to haul him out again, the pelting, freezing rain and Eleanor's laughter washing over them the entire time.

When finally he was above ground, shaking with his shock, the cold, clinging mud and his vicious anger, Henley had ordered his men throw Chelmsford's shrouded corpse into the muddied hole. Then he had simply stalked away, leaving the bare-breasted and bloodied, but now silent, Eleanor kneeling by the mud pit of her husband's grave.

"Mud to mud," she whispered, and lifted her hands into the rain.

Henley dragged his mind back to the present. He reached for his ale cup, then stopped when he realised his hand was shaking too badly to pick it up.

"What is born in mud," she whispered, "returns to mud."

And in a sudden, violent movement, the mistress of Marwood Hagg buried her arms to their elbows in the cold muddied womb of her husband's grave.

Shivering with an unreasoning fear, Henley stumbled down the hall only to halt halfway as one of the midwives hurried towards him from a gap in the screens at the other end.

"My lord! Oh, my dear sweet lord!"

"Lord Christ save us!" Henley muttered, then rushed for the stairs.

She smiled, happy and content, the mistress of Marwood Hagg, and wriggled her arms yet deeper into the mud.

Henley's first impression when he burst into the birthing chamber was that it was freezing.

He halted, so disorientated by the icy atmosphere that for a moment he could do nothing but stand and gape at the scene before him.

In the centre of the room stood the birthing bed, two midwives huddled about it. Both were moaning and wailing and plucking helplessly at the fabric of their aprons.

His wife lay sprawled atop the bed, its linens in jumbled disarray as her hands groped and grasped at her sides.

She was half sitting, her legs bent up and apart, her face looking down to what lay between them.

Henley only gradually realised that she was shrieking, and he shuddered, for her frightful shrieks echoed Eleanor's graveside madness.

There was a clap, as if of thunder, and Henley's eyes jerked to the window.

It was open, its panes swinging wildly in the wind and slamming against the window frame.

Rain gusted through, slicking across the floor with arrow-like determination towards the bed.

Alice shrieked once more, and Henley wrenched his head back towards his wife. She jerked as if trying to escape whatever lay between her legs, but was too weak and hopeless to do anything more than writhe ineffectually.

Something dark and wet issued across the linens, and oozed in clinging fingers down the side of the bed.

Black viscous mud, trickling down to meet the rain-slicked floor.

"*Edmund! Edmund!*" Alice screamed, now half turning towards her husband, one of her hands held out in desperate appeal.

It was black, coated with mud.

Henley took a step forward.

"Witchery," he whispered, his eyes wide and staring.

"Edmund . . . " Alice said again, her voice now a whisper, and her hand dropped back to her side. Her belly, soft and bulbous from the infant it had expelled, rippled and quivered, as if it continued to expel . . .

"Mud!" said Eleanor, her arms still buried in her husband's grave, her sodden hair slinging to her neck and shoulders. "Mud," she said again, and laughed softly.

Henley took the final three steps to his wife's bedside, pushing aside one of the midwives.

The woman slipped in the mud and water on the floor, and fell down with a cry.

Henley had no mind for her. He stared at what lay between his wife's legs . . . and then he, too, moaned.

There lay his son, perfectly formed.

There lay his son, lying in a sea of mud that even now continued to flood forth from his wife's body.

There lay his son, covered in mud, *buried* in mud, mud that bubbled and belched as it poured into the infant's mouth that had opened for its first, life-affirming wail.

His son, silent in his agonising drowning.

His son, staring up at his father with Chelmsford's pale blue terror-struck eyes.

Earth to earth, Henley heard Eleanor's voice whisper in his mind.

He reached down to his son, desperate to rescue him.

Ashes to ashes.

His touched his son's body, and he flinched at the coldness and foulness that coated it.

Dust to dust.

His hands closed about the infant's chest, and his arm muscles contracted as he prepared to lift the child from the death that enveloped it.

Mud to mud.

And then Henley shrieked, for his arms were no longer his, but were the scarlet-clad thin arms of a woman, and her (*his*) long-fingered pale hands were now clasped hatefully about his son, pushing the infant's face deep into the sea of mud, and now there was nothing, nothing but the clumpish, still form of something covered in mud, and the thin scarlet-clad arms buried to the elbows in the mud, and the single bubble, that one single bubble of air that burst hopelessly through the mud with the stink of escaping marsh gas.

The remains of his son's life.

Hundreds of miles north, the woman leaned back and pulled her arms from the grave.

Strangely, her white thin-fingered hands and scarlet-clad arms were unmarked by the mud.

Rain washed in sheets over her, and the wind as it blew chilled her almost to death, but yet still she smiled.

She rose to her feet. "May you *now* finally have peace," she said to the still, cold corpse of her husband buried deep within its embrace of mud.

Then, straight-backed and joyous, the mistress of Marwood Hagg withdrew into her castle.

AUTHOR'S NOTE

This is a nasty story about wifely revenge . . . and a great deal of excess mud. The original title of the story was "Ashes to Ashes, Dust to Dust, Mud to Mud."

BLACK HEART

BLACK HEART

Master William Kempe, physician to the wealthy citizens of thirteenth-century London, stared at the dying youth on the bed and tried to compose his thoughts. There was nothing he could do—the youth was wasted and ashen, no doubt from a growth deep within his body, and no one could aid him now save a Father Confessor.

Kempe swallowed his nervousness and looked at the youth's father standing the other side of the bed. The last thing he wanted to do was inform the Earl of Surrey that his beloved youngest son, Robert, was not long for this world.

"Well?" said the earl. "Why do you not do something?"

"My lord," Kempe said. "I am afraid that there is little I can do. Your son is dying. Perhaps you should call the priest—"

"My son is *not* dying!" the earl shouted. One of his fists clenched slightly, and Kempe did not fail to notice it.

"My lord—"

"Save him, Kempe! I called you to my son's bedside for no other reason!"

"My lord," Kempe repeated as humbly as he might, "I can give the Lord Robert an elixir to dull the pain, but the growth within has so ravaged his flesh that—"

"I do not tolerate failure," the earl said softly, his glacial eyes unblinking on the unhappy Kempe. "Moreover, I do not tolerate failure in a man I *know* has the means to save my son."

Kempe went cold as he suddenly realised what the earl was about to suggest.

"You saved my daughter Matilda when she lay dying in childbed," the earl continued. "Saved her and her infant when all others had given them up to the mercies of the angels. You can do the same now. All you need do is give Robert the same strengthening liquor you gave Matilda."

Kempe lowered his head and studied Robert's wan face once more, offering up a quick prayer to the Virgin Mary that he might find the words to explain to the earl that what had aided Matilda would likely corrupt Robert into something quite monstrous.

The silence between them stretched into a deep uncomfortableness, broken only by Robert's rattling breaths.

"Well?" the earl said eventually.

Kempe raised his eyes to the earl, still glowering at him from the opposite side of the bed.

"My lord, perhaps we might speak outside the chamber?" Kempe indicated the door, and the earl gave a curt nod.

Once the door to the chamber had closed behind them, Kempe began to speak softly, hurriedly and, he hoped, passionately and convincingly.

"My lord, the liquor I gave your daughter—may the saints bless her always—aided her through the final stages of what had been a four day debilitating labour. Her strength was all but gone, and she and the child were almost dead with exhaustion. The strengthening liquor works only for those in the last extremity who need an infusion of courage to defy death and—"

"Then it will be perfect for Robert. *He* needs an infusion of courage needed to defy death."

Now Kempe's voice took on a tone of desperation. "Good sir, it works only for women! To give it to a man would . . . would . . . "

The earl hissed out a word so obscene that Kempe blanched and took an involuntary step back.

"You *will* give this liquor to my son!"

"My lord, it would be counter-productive! It would . . . " *Oh sweet Virgin Mary, how to explain what that heinous liquor would do to his son's heart?*

The earl seized the front of the physician's robe. "If you do not agree to do as I ask, Kempe," he said in a voice low and heavy with menace, "then I cannot vouch for the continued health and safety of *your* son! The streets are so dangerous these days, do you not agree? Young Master Kempe might very well find a knife stuck to its hilt between his ribs one fine day. *Do you understand me, Kempe?*"

Kempe gave one tight, terrified nod, and the earl let him go.

"I will expect you back here this evening with the liquor, Kempe. If my son dies, then so does yours."

And with that he was gone, leaving the physician shaking with fear in his wake.

By the time Kempe had walked back to his house on Lambert Hill red-hot anger had replaced his fear. How dare the earl so threaten him? How *dare* the earl not listen to his physician's advice? Kempe was sorry now he'd ever saved Matilda, and even more sorry he'd mentioned the special liquor to her father. Normally Kempe spoke of it only as an ordinary herbal brew . . . but in Matilda's case Kempe had unadvisedly bragged of the uniqueness of the liquor to the earl.

Now look to what troubles his boasting had brought him!

Kempe entered his house, walked through to the kitchen, and caught his wife Margery's eye. Then he looked to the two apprentices working at cutting up herbs on the table, then to the door, then, finally, to the cellar.

She nodded slightly, understanding, and turned to the apprentices as Kempe opened the door to the cellar stairwell, lighting the oil lamp that hung at the top of the stairs before making his way down.

He had to wait only a few minutes before he heard the apprentices leave the building. The door to the cellar opened, and Margery climbed down the steps to join him.

"We won't be disturbed?" Kempe said.

"No," Margery said. "I've sent the two boys off to Master Osmond's to purchase some new vials. They will be gone two hours or more. Our son won't be home until the evening. My dear? What is wrong?"

"Trouble, Margery. Trouble." He told her of what had passed between himself and the Earl of Surrey, and Margery's face paled.

"But you cannot give young Lord Robert the liquor, William! It is safe only on those women in the extremity of childbirth! They sweat out its potency in the agony of their labour . . . while Robert will absorb it into the very fabric of his being."

"Yes, yes, I know." It wasn't only that labouring women sweated out the majority of the liquor's potency—women's natural sweetness and compassion negated what little of the dark liquor remained within their systems. In Robert, the liquor would not only be absorbed in its entirety, but would also magnify the youth's male aggression and anger.

"And," Margery continued, "we have so little left!"

Kempe grimaced. Ah, the very crux of the matter. There was almost nothing remaining of that very peculiar ingredient they needed to make the liquor. Kempe, as his father and grandfather before him, was renowned for his ability to bring even the weakest woman through childbirth when other physicians routinely lost at least a third of their mothers. But then, those other physicians didn't have what Kempe (as his father and grandfather) had, did they?

Unwillingly, Kempe found his eyes drawn to the secret door at the back of the cellar, behind which stood the barrel containing . . . well, containing that which his grandfather had brought home from the Holy Land almost ninety years earlier.

"We have enough to last us another year," Margery said very softly, also now looking towards the secret door. "No more. Then I do not know what we will do. William, we *cannot* afford to waste even a fraction of our precious remnant on Robert!"

Margery was no longer concerned so much about what might happen to Robert, but that his dose would mean one less successful childbirth miracle for her husband. One less grateful husband to pay whatever her husband demanded.

Kempe did not answer. Instead he walked slowly across the cellar, and hooked his finger into the hidden catch that made a section of shelving slide out to reveal the small chamber behind it. Only he and Margery knew of this chamber; not Kempe's apprentices, and not even his own son. If their supplies ran out there would never be a need to reveal to his son the cellar's vile secret.

Both Kempe and Margery, now at her husband's shoulder, gagged a little at the stench that flowed out to meet them. No matter how many times they entered this chamber, they never got used to the smell.

The chamber contained nothing but a large cask, tarred and waxed to make it waterproof, and a small stone-topped table on which was set several knives, a pair of tongs, and a pestle and mortar. Kempe handed the lamp to Margery, then stepped forward to the cask, steeling himself as he slid off its lid.

The oily black liquid inside stirred gently, even though Kempe had not caused the cask to move. Something rose to the surface, breaking through the liquid with a horrible wet bubbling sound, then bobbed gently on the surface as if waiting for Kempe's hand.

It was a blackened, swollen piece of meat, rotted beyond all possible recognition.

"Our last piece," Margery whispered, staring over Kempe's shoulder. "Our very last piece."

"Aye," Kempe said.

The very last piece indeed—the last remnant of a human heart, the remaining fragment of the fourteen hearts his grandfather had brought back from the Holy Land.

The wicked, hateful hearts that had become the cornerstone of his grandfather's, then his father's, and now his own extraordinary success at saving women who would otherwise have died in childbirth. It had made them rich . . . and now soon the final precious piece would be just that bit smaller.

Its preciousness wasted on damned Robert!

Kempe stared at the rotting piece of heart bobbing its repellent way about the surface of the black preserving liquid, remembering the tale of its acquisition. Ninety-two years ago his grandfather had gone on crusade and had been present during one of the bleakest and most depraved episodes of crusading history. A band of fourteen crusader knights had gone berserk, attacking innocent women and children for the sheer joy of feeling their swords slice through tender, defenceless flesh. The fourteen knights had murdered over one hundred women and children before a force of some sixty knights, appalled at what their brothers were doing, tried to stop them.

Depraved these fourteen knights may have been, but their strength and courage and tenacity was astounding. Of the sixty knights who tried to stop the murderers, only twenty-one remained alive by the time the fourteen black-hearted knights were themselves dead.

Kempe's grandfather, intrigued by the strength and bravery of these fourteen admittedly contemptible men, managed to steal their hearts from their corpses while they lay unguarded before their burial. He'd learned from Arab physicians that the dead flesh of someone who had been particularly strong could be used to impart strength to the still-living. And so he had preserved the hearts in a cask filled with a liquid composed of part alcohol, part spices and part oils, and set sail for England.

Back in London, Kempe's grandfather had experimented with slices of pulverised heart in his medicines—quickly learning that the only people the dark heart liquor could be given safely to were labouring women.

Anyone else who drank of the dark murderous hearts became dark and murderous themselves, as evil as the crusaders who had attacked the innocent.

And so had been founded the Kempe physicians' extraordinary reputation for guiding even the weakest of women through childbirth. Their wealth and success was founded entirely on those fourteen depraved hearts . . . and now they were all but gone.

"My dear," Margery said, her voice so sudden in the silence of the chamber that Kempe literally jumped, "I have an idea."

He turned slightly to look at her, frowning a little at the excitement in her eyes.

She smiled, and it was a cold and nasty thing. "I think that there might be a way to satisfy my Earl of Surrey's demands *and* restock our supply. A way," the tip of her tongue ran delicately over her top lip, "to ensure the continuation of your successful practice for years to come. Of course, poor Robert shall have to pay a heavy price."

"Yes?" Kempe said.

Every last vestige of the earl's threatening demeanour vanished the instant Kempe arrived back at his palace.

"I cannot thank you enough!" he exclaimed as he escorted the physician to his son's sick bed.

Kempe merely smiled, and clasped the vial of liquor a little more closely to his chest. Margery and he had sliced a fragment of flesh from what remained of the final heart, pulverising it and then dissolving it in a sweet spiced potion, finishing their work well before either the apprentices or their son had returned home. Now, hope in his own vile heart, Kempe was feeling quite kindly towards the earl.

His smile stretched a little further, then he unstoppered the flask and bent to the dying youth.

The rejuvenating effect was almost immediate as the courage and strength imparted from the juices of the crusader's dark heart filtered through Robert's system. Within moments of Kempe dripping some of the liquor between the youth's thin, white lips, Robert's eyes fluttered open and he took a deep, surprised breath.

"Father!" he exclaimed, and struggled into a sitting position.

"Have some more," Kempe said, holding the vial to the youth's lips.

The earl laughed, even as tears of joy ran down his cheeks.

Within two weeks the earl's joy had turned to bleak despair. Robert had risen from his death bed within a day, and had returned into the full bloom of health within a mere three days after that.

But . . . the youth had changed. Where once was kindness and courtesy was now vileness and antagonism. Nothing, not even his father's shouting, could restrain the lad. He began to roam London's streets at night, ignoring curfews and evading the night watchmen. One night the battered corpse of a woman was found slumped against the back wall of St Paul's, the next night two children were found torn apart under one of the wharves on the Thames. Then one of the night watches was attacked by a single assailant: five men were slaughtered within the space of a few moments while the unknown assailant slid away into the blackness of London's night.

Kempe, knowing full well who it was, carried on with his duties attending the ill, a bland smile on his face.

At night, he ensured that his entire family, including his apprentices, stayed safe inside his well-locked and shuttered house.

The murders and horror continued until, one night, a force of forty-seven men-at-arms cornered the youthful, black-hearted Robert in a blind courtyard. There they attacked him, thinking of all the innocents he had slaughtered in the previous nights. Robert, his natural courage augmented by the audacity and daring of the black crusader's heart, kept them at bay for almost half an hour, using his sword and a pike with murderous efficiency against the men-at-arms.

Eleven of them died before Robert's strength finally gave out, and he slipped on the night-dampened cobbles, his sword clattering from his hand.

Instantly the men-at-arms swarmed over him, their blades flashing in the moonlight.

"Master Kempe," the earl said, his voice full of grief and horror, "thank you for attending."

Kempe nodded, arranging his features into an expression of sorrow. The earl stood before a trestle table in his son's chamber.

Across its top stretched the mutilated corpse of Robert.

"I wanted . . . I thought . . . this is so hideous . . . " The earl could not continue, and he turned away, lest the physician see the tears in his eyes.

"You would like me to stitch his dear flesh back together again, that he may meet his Maker in one piece?" murmured Kempe.

The earl nodded. "If . . . if you would be so kind. Thank you. Kempe . . . Kempe, oh sweet Jesu, I should have listened to you!"

Kempe thought it best to drop his eyes, and fold his hands before him.

Eventually the earl regained some semblance of emotional control. He took a deep breath, asked Kempe if he had everything he wanted, then left the physician alone with the corpse.

As the door closed behind him, Kempe raised his face, finally allowing his triumphant smile full flower.

Clutching his bag of instruments, and re-checking that he was alone in the chamber, Kempe approached the corpse.

It was covered in sword wounds—in some places the flesh had been virtually shredded from his ribcage.

"Good," Kempe whispered, "for this shall make my small intrusion all the more unnoticeable."

He set his bag of instruments up on a side table, opening it and selecting a pair of retractors and a saw.

Then he set to, working as quickly and as cleanly as he could, opening the youth's ribcage and exposing his heart.

His black, corrupted heart.

Kempe grinned, and snipped the tendons and blood vessels that connected the heart to its surrounding tissues until it lay free in his hands.

It was cold and slimy, and its black flesh stank.

But Kempe nodded, pleased, and slipped the heart into a waterproof pouch which he secreted within his bag of instruments. Later he would take it down to the secret chamber, and slide it into the cask of preserving liquid.

Restocked, his lucrative practice at the sides of labouring women would be safe for a few years yet.

And when stocks ran low again, well, Kempe was sure he would be able to engineer another monstrous black-hearted murderer from whom he could reap another corrupted heart.

He was well served in his wife, indeed.

Whistling cheerily, Kempe set to stitching poor murderous Robert back into some semblance of prettiness for his burial.

ST UNCUMBER

ST UNCUMBER

Mistress Mathilda Kempe walked slowly down the narrow laneway, her feet scuffing the cobbles in her exhaustion. She stopped momentarily at the end of the lane, leaning against a wall as she gathered her strength, then moved off again, trying to pick up her pace. Her husband, Ormond, would be impatient for her return, and likely to grow angrier with every moment of her delay.

Crossing Cheapside, medieval London's principal market thoroughfare and busy even at this early hour, Mathilda wearily shifted her bag of instruments from one hand to the other. She'd spent all night midwiving for one of her regular customers—Mistress Goodall. This had been the woman's fifth birth, and while all had gone well, Mathilda was worn out after the long night spent at the mother's side.

She must ensure she rested well today. Another of her expectant mothers, Mistress Joanna Mercer, was due to deliver very soon. Unlike Mistress Goodall, however, Joanna faced an extraordinarily difficult birth: she was a tiny birdlike woman carrying a large and badly presented baby, and weak after suffering a debilitating fever two weeks previously. Mathilda doubted that even her midwiving skills could save the woman.

And nothing will save me, she thought, picking up her pace even more, *if I do not make haste to my husband.*

"Where have you been?"

Ormond was waiting for her inside the back door that led directly into their kitchen. His rotund face was flushed and shining, his bright blue eyes were screwed up, and his solid bulk was shifting impatiently from foot to foot.

Ormond was furious, and Mathilda took a deep breath, praying she could deflect the worst of his anger.

"Ormond, I am sorry. I could not leave Mistress Goodall until well past dawn. I made haste as best I could, but—"

"Have you not thought of the business I have lost while you have been playing the laggard? I could have made fifteen sales in the time you have taken to get home."

"There was no need for you to wait for me," Mathilda said. *Merciful Virgin, she was going to collapse if she didn't sit down soon!*

"*Someone* had to be here!" Ormond shouted, and Mathilda flinched at the expression on his face, taking a defensive step backward until her back pressed against the closed outer door.

"The bone merchant is due here this morning with new supplies," Ormond said. "I *need* those bones. I can't risk Simon Helft just wandering off if there isn't someone here to pay him."

If Ormond hadn't already managed to spoil Mathilda's day, then mention of the repulsive Simon Helft certainly did. The ancient bone merchant was a hateful man. It wasn't merely his physical appearance that nauseated Mathilda—yellow wizened features, cold papery skin and an over-large red tongue that permanently flickered in the corners of his fleshy lips—but also his choleric temper, a match for Ormond's own. Mathilda felt sympathy (and empathy) with Helft's wife, Hawise, for having to live out her days with such a repellent man.

Somehow Mathilda managed a smile. "I will be here for the bone merchant, Ormond. I promise." *Just go and leave me*, she thought. *Please. Just go.* "I have been a poor wife in being so late and delaying you, and I am sorry for that."

Somewhat mollified, Ormond nodded, then moved to the table where stood a large backpack. It was full of tiny pottery vials full of the potions he sold, and it clinked as she lifted it onto his back.

"I will do good business today," he said.

Indeed, he very probably would, Mathilda thought. Ormond claimed to be a trained physician, and sold potions which he said contained pulverised portions of various saints' bones. A potion containing a fragment of pulverised bone dust from St Claire for those suffering from poor eyesight, a potion of St Roch for those suffering from fever and boils, St Cosmus for botches and biles, St Apolline for rotting teeth, St Agatha for those with sore breasts. For every complaint Ormond had a vial containing the appropriate saintly bone dust dissolved into a honeyed potion.

For the very ill (but also very rich), Ormond even had a clotted white substance which he claimed to be the milk of the Virgin Mary.

The truth was that Ormond had barely learned to read or write, let alone undergo an apprenticeship with a trained physician, and Mathilda suspected that the bones he purchased from Simon Helft were nothing more than fragments of cattle and pig bones. As for the Virgin Mary's 'milk', well, Mathilda knew for a fact that Ormond made that from goat's cheese.

But what could she do? Mathilda's midwifery business paid little, and she depended on Ormond for the roof over her head and the food that she ate. She'd married Ormond several years ago thinking that he was what he claimed, and the slow discovery that he was nothing but a charlatan as a physician and a thin-tempered despot as a husband had stripped away the last of her naïve innocence.

Several times a week Mathilda thanked sweet Jesus that they had no children, for Ormond would doubtless prove an even worse father than he was a husband.

"Make sure you do as I ask," Ormond said. "I am almost out of bone."

Mathilda nodded, wishing that he'd just go, then managed to force a loving—yet submissive—smile to her face as Ormond shot her a black look.

"God keep you safe," she said.

Ormond stared an instant longer, then brushed past, opened the door, and was gone.

Mathilda briefly closed her eyes in the sudden blessed relief of his absence, then walked over to the chair by the fire, stumbling slightly in her weariness.

She sank down, resting her head against the chair's high back. She tried to empty her mind, and while she was successful so far as Ormond was concerned, she was not so successful with her continuing nagging worry over Joanna Mercer's forthcoming labour.

Mathilda stared unseeing at the rack of pans that hung across from her. Joanna had no chance at all, and the thought that she would be able to do nothing for the woman but bear witness to her slow struggle into death depressed Mathilda deeply.

She decided she might as well rise and begin the day's chores when there was a sudden loud knock at the door.

Mathilda jumped, her heart thudding. *Simon Helft!*

She hesitated, then steeled herself, determined not to allow the man to upset her.

But it was not Simon Helft at all. Rather, there stood Hawise, Helft's aging wife, with a bright and cheerful smile on her normally taciturn face.

"Mistress Hawise?" Mathilda said, looking about to see if Helft was loitering in the laneway.

"Indeed, 'tis Mistress Hawise," the woman said. If anything, her smile had grown broader at Mathilda's obvious confusion.

"Where is your husband?" Mathilda said. "Ormond needs a new stock of bones. Badly. Is—"

"Simon is gone," said Hawise, "and so are his bones. You'll get just me this day."

"But Ormond needs those bones!"

Hawise studied Mathilda's face, correctly interpreting the reason for the young woman's fear. *Poor girl,* she thought, *Mathilda's husband is almost as vile as mine had been.*

"My dear," Hawise said gently, "may I speak a moment, and explain? Simon left six days ago, having decided to undertake a pilgrimage to convert the heathen Mongols at the court of Genghis Khan."

Mathilda stared at Hawise in complete shock. The land of Genghis Khan? But that lay beyond the known world in the all but mythical Cathay. No one travelled there and returned!

"Of course," Hawise continued, her eyes twinkling, "I can't imagine that the terrible Genghis Khan will treat poor Simon kindly."

"But . . . *why?*"

Hawise shrugged. "How can any woman know the strange convolutions of a man's mind, my dear? Simon decided to go, and, as the good and obedient wife, I could only bow to his wishes."

"But . . . " Mathilda was still having trouble trying to accept what Hawise was saying. Helft had gone, and there were no bones for Ormond?

"I have decided to travel to Lincoln to live with my eldest daughter and her husband," Hawise continued. "She shall be glad enough to see me, I think."

"But what will Ormond do without his bones?" Mathilda said. Ormond's anger was the only thing she could think of.

"There, there, my dear. They were only pig's bones, as I am sure you were well enough aware. Do not fret about your husband—"

Easy enough for her to say, Mathilda thought wretchedly.

"—for I have a gift for you." Hawise rolled back a sleeve, and took from her arm a plain copper bangle. Its only distinguishing feature was a curious design that wound about its length.

"A wise woman gave this to me a week ago," Hawise said, slipping the bangle on to Mathilda's unresisting arm, "and now I think it is time for you to wear it. It is said that this is the bangle from the arm of the saintly Uncumber, may the angels bless her always. Use it well and wisely, my dear."

She leaned forward and kissed Mathilda's cheek. "Now I must be off. 'Tis a long journey to Lincoln and I cannot linger here."

After Hawise had gone Mathilda returned to her seat by the fire, a hand absently toying with St Uncumber's bangle about her arm. *There were no more bones for Ormond? What would he say? What would he do?*

She wondered if she could take the pennies Ormond had left for Helft's bones and hurry to the market to see if the butchers had any old bones in their refuse heaps. But what if they told Ormond? Worse, what if he saw her?

Eventually she decided to do nothing but somehow weather Ormond's fury when he returned. And so Mathilda sat by the kitchen fire, completely still, her eyes staring unseeing ahead, and waited through the rest of the morning and the afternoon for her husband to return.

She cursed the day Helft had ever thought to leave on such a fruitless pilgrimage.

At sunset hurried footsteps approached the back door.

Ormond! Mathilda sprang from her chair, her heart thudding.

But instead of coming straight through the door, whoever was the other side stopped, and tapped upon it softly.

Still frightened (but yet relieved that this obviously was not Ormond), Mathilda managed to collect herself enough to open the door, and receive her second surprise for the day.

It was Brother Frances, the priest who served her local parish church of St Mary-le-Bow.

"Brother Frances?" Mathilda said, wondering if she had somehow forgotten to pay her tithes, for she could imagine no other reason for the man's visit.

"Mistress Kempe," said the priest, "may I come in? I have . . . I have heavy news."

Mathilda stepped back and gestured the priest to take the chair by the fire while she drew up a stool.

When they were seated she studied the priest closely. His face was flushed and sweating, and his normally bland brown eyes bright with emotion.

Brother Frances leaned forward, and took both Mathilda's hands in his. "Mistress, you have heard of the zealots who, inspired by our crusaders' recent victories in the Holy Lands, declared their intention to fit out a ship and sail to the very edge of the world, there to convert the fairies and elves which live there?"

Deeply puzzled, for she did not know how this could concern her, Mathilda nodded. "They said they'd been visited with visions from the saints who told them that this voyage would ensure the salvation of their souls."

"Aye. Well, their ship sailed on the noon tide. And, I am saddened to say, Ormond sailed with it."

"*What?*" Mathilda sat back, pulling her hands from the priest's grip.

"Ormond had gone down to Tower Wharf to sell his wares this morning," the priest said.

No doubt, thought Mathilda, *for the disease-ridden sailors who haunted Tower Wharf always bought generously of Ormond's fakery.*

"Then, suddenly, in the late morning," Brother Frances continued, "Ormond had a fit. He fell to the ground, his limbs jiggling, his mouth foaming. Several people ran to his aid, but when they finally managed to get him to his feet, Ormond threw off their concern. He shouted to all who could hear that he'd had a vision from Saint Uncumber, who had told him that wealth and fame would be his if he sailed with the zealots."

Mathilda, her mouth hanging open, was unable to say anything.

"My dear . . . no one could stop him. He instantly offered his services as a physician to the zealots, and they accepted. The ship sailed before anyone could dissuade Ormond from his course—"

Mathilda uncharitably wondered if anyone had tried particularly hard.

"—or before I could hurry to the wharf to add my pleas to theirs. Mistress Kempe, I am sorry. I doubt anyone could have stopped Ormond from his course of action."

Mathilda was silent long minutes, digesting what Brother Frances had told her. Ormond, gone to sail to the edge of the world to convert fairies . . . just as Helft had set off to convert the barbarous warriors at the court of Genghis Khan.

She fingered the bangle about her arm. "Brother . . . who is this St Uncumber who visited Ormond with a vision?"

He shrugged a little. "A minor saint, and of a dubious heritage. Some women claim she aids her fellow sisters in disencumbering them of their burdens." He looked at Mathilda sharply. "*You have not been praying to her, have you?*"

"No," Mathilda said. "I have not. Today is the first time I have heard St Uncumber's name."

Brother Frances nodded, satisfied with the truth of her statement. "Then I think that we should spend some time in prayer, Mistress Kempe, to ensure that your husband truly achieves the salvation he deserves."

That evening Joanna Mercer, the tiny woman Mathilda so feared for, went into labour. Mathilda hurried to Joanna's side the instant she received summons from Joanna's husband, William, and set about doing what she could for the labouring woman.

As she had feared, it was not much.

Within hours Joanna was in agony, the baby was unshiftable, and the birthing chamber stank of death.

Mathilda, trying to keep a calm demeanour, was nevertheless distraught. Joanna and her husband, William, were kind and generous people, and enjoyed a loving marriage. They'd longed for this child, even though both were well aware of the risks. It was not fair that such sweetness and love should end this way . . . especially when she, Mathilda, had miraculously found herself released from such an unhappy marriage this same day.

Mathilda, watching helplessly as Joanna struggled and writhed, suddenly realised she was toying absently with the copper bangle of St Uncumber. *Some women claim she aids her fellow sisters in disencumbering them of their burdens,* Brother Frances had said. Mathilda's breath suddenly caught in her throat: what if such burdens might not be exclusively spousal?

Use it well and wisely, Hawise had told her.

Mathilda twisted the bangle from her own arm and slipped it about Joanna's. "Saint Uncumber," she muttered, "I beg you, free Joanna of her encumbrance as you have freed Hawise and myself!"

Joanna gave a sudden start, and her mouth opened wide in disbelief. "Mathilda!" she whispered, "Mathilda!"

And then she gave a great gasp, and bore down with all her might.

An hour later Mathilda opened the door of the birthing chamber and beckoned an anxious William inside. "A daughter," she said, "and as fair as your own wife."

And then she smiled, one of her hands toying with the copper bangle once again about her own arm.

Within three months Mathilda had the busiest midwifery practice in London. Of the five score women she had aided during these three months, all had been delivered quickly and easily of healthy infants.

And of those five score women, eight had husbands who, during the course of their wives' labours, quite suddenly and inexplicably decided to embark that very moment upon long and dangerous pilgrimages, all to the very ends of the earth.

Strangely, none of those eight wives seemed particularly distraught at their husbands' abrupt departures.

Suddenly husbandless or not, all the new mothers thanked Mathilda effusively, grateful for her assistance in a world where a fifth of all women died in childbed.

Mathilda accepted their gratitude with due grace. Of the fees she collected, half she donated to a charity in aid of abandoned wives, always in the name of St Uncumber.

Wisely and well was a motto Mathilda kept to the end of her days.

THE EVIL WITHIN

THE EVIL WITHIN

This world, this wasteland, lies heavy with evil. Here writhe
serpents, here sting pests, here rot grub worms, here raven
wolves, here sin issues in glistening rivulets from the mouths of
the dead. Here evil roams on the breath of wind and the dance of
dust motes, here evil shrouds itself in the shadows of earth clods
and the cavities of human bodies. Here live men and women, the
sinful fruit of Adam's weak loins and Eve's vile womb. For her
sin, they are condemned to this wasteland, to their toil in the
dust, to their scratchings at the boil of plague and the bite of pest.
Here, amid all this wretchedness, lies the seed of their salvation
and the terror of their damnation: battle the evil without and
conquer the sin within; succumb to the evil without, and suffer
the worms of Hell for all eternity.

Here, this world, this wasteland.

It was an age of gloom and despondency. The population
of Europe lay decimated by the creeping pestilence, forests
encroached upon untended fields, wolves ranged into villages,
and the darkness crept down from the mountain slopes even at
the crest of the noonday sun.

Night was an abomination, the haunt of demons and devils, incubi and sharp-toothed fairies, and black ravening dogs that had no place on God's earth. Screeches and howls wailed through the most tightly shuttered window, and the most carefully tended infant was vulnerable to forces unnameable.

Hell incarnate roamed abroad, and no pathway was safe, no barred home a haven.

Especially not from the evil within.

His hands stiff with cold, Friar Arnaud Courtete wrapped his cloak a little more tightly about him and slowly raised his eyes into the wind. Before him a narrow trail wound upwards about the grey mountainside before disappearing into the uncertainty of low rain clouds.

Should he continue? The day was half gone already, and the village of Gebetz an afternoon's walk away. But Arques was already a day behind him, and Courtete had no wish to spend another night in the open.

Besides, he could not turn back. Bishop Fournier would not be pleased.

"Holy Virgin, guide my steps," Courtete mumbled, one hand fumbling at the cross about his neck, and then hefted his staff and stepped forward.

Although Fournier had no jurisdiction over Courtete's mendicant order, he was a powerful and influential bishop, and when he had asked Courtete to visit Gebetz, the friar had little option of refusal.

But Gebetz!

Courtete been there several times in the past, but that had been years ago, and he'd been a young man, both his body and spirit strong. Now his age made his footsteps falter, and a lifetime of priestly asceticism battling frail human need had left his spirit vulnerable.

Courtete hoped he had the faith to endure whatever he might find in Gebetz.

"The priest there is young," Fournier had told Courtete. "Inexperienced and idealistic. A fatal combination in these malignant days. I have heard Gebetz is troubled."

"And if it is 'troubled'?" Courtete had asked the bishop.

"Then send down the mountain to me for Guillaume Maury. I will send him. And his pack."

Gebetz might only be a small and poor village, but it was strategically positioned, straddling the high trails of the northern Pyrenees. If Gebetz succumbed to godless forces, then the trails would be closed, no man would be able to drive his sheep into the rich summer pastures, nor no pilgrim wend his way to Santiago. The mountain passes would be lost to Christendom forever more.

It was the only reason Fournier was willing to even entertain the idea of letting Maury and his pack move so far from the cathedral.

Courtete shuddered, and hoped that Gebetz wasn't so besieged that it needed Maury and his creatures. Courtete wasn't sure what he feared more—evil in whatever form it took, or Maury and his fiendish spawn.

But was there any difference?

"Holy Virgin, Mother of God," he whispered, "light my way, guide my feet, cradle my soul, save me, save me, save me . . . "

As Courtete climbed further into the mountains, strange shapes danced in and out of the shadows of his wake. Some took the form of fish with the jointed legs of locusts, others were formed like creatures of the earth, but with perverted elongated or scaled forms and the slavering jaws of nightmares. Still more creatures were vaguely man-like, save for odd horns, or extra limbs, or the half-lumped flesh of the graveyard.

All faded into the mist whenever Courtete spun about, his eyes wild.

The dusk had gathered and Courtete's limbs were shaking with exhaustion and fear by the time he rounded the final bend into Gebetz. He stopped, his breath tight in his chest, and looked down from the trail to where the village nestled in the hollow formed by the convergence of three mountains.

It was still, silent.

Had darkness won, then?

Courtete gripped his staff tighter and fought the urge to run.

Run where? Night was falling, and he was in the mountains!

Above him a bell pealed, and Courtete cried out. He spun around, frantically looking about him, his staff falling from nerveless hands.

An icy wind whistled between the mountains, lifting his robe and cloak so that the coarse material wrapped itself about his head, obscuring his vision and stifling his breathing.

Courtete's hands scrabbled desperately until he freed his face, his eyes darting about to spot the demon that had attacked him.

Nothing. No-one.

Gebetz lay still and silent.

Even the chimneys were smokeless.

Courtete's hand groped for his cross, and he steadied his breathing.

The bell pealed again, and this time Courtete heard a foreboding mumble follow it.

"*Where are you?*" he screamed, his hand now so tightly gripped about his cross its edges cut into his flesh. "*Come forth and face me!*"

Again the peal, much closer now, and a rumble of voice sounded with it.

"Who are you?" Courtete whispered this time, sure that demons slid down the mountain sides towards him, hidden by the gloom and mist.

A light flared some fifteen paces above him, and Courtete's eyes jerked towards it.

The bell pealed again, frantic itself now, as if whoever—whatever—held it had succumbed to the jerking madness, and a rabble of voices rose in the mist.

"Lord God, Redeemer!"

"Bloodied Jesus!"

"Holy Virgin—"

"Save us! Save us! Save us!"

Courtete slowly let his breath out in relief. It was the villagers who were above him, and no doubt the young priest Bernard Planissole who wielded the bell.

"Holy Redeemer—"

"Crucified God—"

"Drive evil from our homes—"

"And from our fields—"

"And from the paths of the shepherds!"

The bell tolled again, far closer, and Courtete jumped yet again. Holy Mother, he thought, they are engaged in a Perambulation Against Evil!

Was it *this* bad?

Without warning a black figure jumped down from the mist onto the road before Courtete. It was a young, wild-eyed man, black-robed in the service of Christ. In one hand he carried a bell, in the other a spluttering, smoking torch.

He thrust both in Courtete's face, the bell shrieking and bellowing.

"Get you gone!" the priest screamed. "In the name of God, and of the Son . . . and . . . and . . . "

"And by the Virgin, Planissole!" Courtete said, recovering his own clerical composure and the authority of his age in the presence of the young priest's panic. "Can you not see that *I* walk in Christ's footsteps, too?"

And he held forth the small cross from his neck.

Planissole abruptly stopped yelling, although he still tolled the bell. He stared at Courtete, wet black hair plastered across his forehead, green eyes startling in a white face, the flesh of his cheeks trembling, a sodden robe clinging to a thin body.

"I am Friar Arnaud Courtete," Courtete said, extending his hand. "Here to aid you and strengthen God's word in this sorrowful place."

Other figures now stepped out of the undergrowth and mist to stand behind Planissole. Without exception they were stark-eyed and gaunt-cheeked, their faces contorted with the trials of sleepless nights, their clothes clinging damply to bodies shaking with fear, the pale skin of their faces and hands smudged with grime and fatigue, their mouths still moving with invocation and prayer, although no sound issued forth.

Save us, save us, save us!

"Planissole," Courtete said as evenly as he could manage, "will you tell me what is wrong?"

Planissole stared, then dropped the bell, put his hands to his face, and began to keen, a thin wail of fear that echoed about the mountains.

The bell rolled over the edge of the trail and bounced down the side of the hill, jangling and clamouring, until it landed in a small gutter that ran beside a row of houses.

There it lay half submerged in grey-streaked sewage, its tongue finally silenced.

Planissole led Courtete through the village, the villagers trailing behind them in a muttering, jittery crowd. Planissole's eyes never ceased to move right and left as they walked, and Courtete found his heart thudding violently every time the breeze billowed the mist about them. Yet he maintained an outward composure, for surely Planissole and his flock were close to a fateful panic. Finally they drew close to the great stone church that stood at the far end of the village. There was nothing beyond the church, save a trail that led yet further into the uncertainty of the mist and mountains.

Planissole saw Courtete study the trail. "No-one has come down that trail for the past week," he said. "And yet there must still be shepherds and pilgrims trapped in the mountains. Dead. Or worse."

Courtete turned from the trail to Father Planissole, but thought it wisest to say nothing, and after a moment the priest led him inside the church.

It was a large, substantial and well-appointed church, catering for the transient population of shepherds and pilgrims as well as villagers. A beautifully carved rood screen separated altar from nave, and carvings of the saints, apostles and of the vices and virtues adorned the sixteen pillars supporting the roof. The windows were small, but beautifully blocked with stained glass, and the walls and roof had been plastered and then painted with stories of the bible.

The smell of roasting pig was entirely out of character.

Planissole's thin face assumed an expression of fretful guilt as he saw Courtete stare at the pig spitted above a fire towards the rear of the nave.

"Forgive our insult to our Lord and the Saints," Planissole said, "but for the past eight days and nights the entire population of the village has lived in this church. It is better protected against the foes of the night. Of necessity we must cook in here as well."

Courtete graced the man with a smile, and waved a vague absolution for the sacrilege.

The villagers had crowded in behind the two priests, and Planissole and Courtete stepped to one side to give them room. Some sank down to rest on piles of bedding heaped amid scattered baskets behind the pillars, several women moved to the fire, setting prepared pots of food among the coals, and the rest grouped about the two priests.

"It is too dangerous to live beyond these sanctified walls?" Courtete asked.

Planissole nodded. "Will you sit?" He waved to the warmth of the fire and they settled down, the villagers spread in a respectful circle about them. "Let me tell you our story."

Even as he took breath to speak, there was a thump on the roof, and an unearthly wailing from beyond the walls.

"Night has fallen," said a woman some paces away, and she hurriedly crossed herself.

"*Evil* has fallen," Planissole said softly, and then he began his tale.

It was far worse than Courtete had feared. The corruption had struck four weeks previously, growing progressively stronger with each night and feeding off the fear and helplessness of the villagers.

The village dogs had been the first to sense the demonic onslaught.

"They fled one night," Planissole said to Courtete. The priest had calmed now the church doors were safely bolted, and Courtete realised that he spoke very well for a simple parish priest. Too well, perhaps. Almost bespeaking an education beyond that of most mountain clerics.

"After the Sabbath sunset the dogs began howling," Planissole continued, not realising Courtete's interest in him, "then they ran into the streets, growling and screaming and speaking in strange—"

"*Speaking?*" Courtete said.

"Speaking," Planissole repeated softly. "They spoke in a language I have never heard before, but which I now believe to be the tongue of Lucifer's minions. After the passage of the first part of the night they massed and fled into the night . . . into the mountains."

"Up the trail that extends beyond this church?" Courtete asked, and Planissole nodded.

"From that night on we have been visited by terror. Great winds that have lifted the roofs of houses and torn the babes from their mother's arms. Food has rotted within an hour of being cooked, and worms have wriggled from bread freshly baked and broken. Great . . . " Planissole took a deep breath, and forced himself to continue. "Two days ago great cracks appeared in the fields, and from them periodically has issued the sulphurous stench of Hell."

"Mother Mary of Jesus!" Courtete cried, "say it is not so!"

"The rents in the earth have deepened, and now they snake close to the village. Out of them crawl abominations."

"Father," one of the village women said, "our priest relates only the truth, and only a part of what we have had to endure. Look at us!" She swept an arm about the assembled gathering. "We fear to venture out at night—t'would be madness to even think of it!—and during the day we walk the streets and field with our elbows tucked tight against our bodies lest we bump the ghosts who throng about!"

A middle-aged man, his clothes hanging about his thin frame all patched and worn, his face weather-beaten, his eyes dull, now stepped forth and spoke. "And yet what this village endures is paradise compared to the inferno that burns within the mountain passes."

"And you are?" Courtete asked.

"My name is Jaques. I am a shepherd. I wander the mountain trails with my sheep, searching for sweet pasture and a dry place to lay down at night. But . . . forgive me, Father . . . I cannot speak of it."

"Jaques, and several other shepherds struggled out of the mountains nine nights ago," Planissole said. "They were wild with fear. They said that a great dark shape that shrieked and wailed ate their sheep, and while it was so occupied, they fled. They'd run for three days and two nights, not stopping, not daring to."

"And no-one else has come down from the mountains?" Courtete said, thinking that the dogs had fled *into* the mountains. Was that where the evil was concentrated? *What had they gone to meet?*

"Only one man," Planissole said, and indicated a curly black-haired young man wrapped in a dark cloak sitting against one of the pillars. "A pilgrim. Winding his way home from St James of Santiago de Compostella. He arrived five nights ago. Maybe the Saint protected him through the mountains, for none have followed him out."

Courtete stared at the man, who nodded politely. He was reasonably well-dressed, but not ostentatiously. A staff and pilgrim's scrip lay on the floor next to him, and Courtete noticed that there were several badges on the shoulders of the man's cloak. He'd been travelling a while to have collected so many pilgrim badges, and Courtete thought he was probably the son of a merchant or minor nobleman, on pilgrimage to atone for some youthful escapade.

Courtete looked about at the fear-worn faces of the villages, and listened to the howlings and rappings outside.

"Wait here," he said, laying a hand on Planissole's shoulder, and he rose and walked with heavy heart to a small window in the back wall of the nave that normally framed the deformed faces of lepers too contagious to be allowed inside for mass.

Now the glass revealed something more horrible even than the contagion of leprosy.

A creature, half donkey, half man, was careering in and out of the thickening mist. Part of one malformed limb had been eaten away.

As frightful as that creature was, to one side something else caught Courtete's attention, and he pressed his face closer to the glass.

A black imp with thin shoulders, grotesque pot belly, and overly-large hands and feet squatted on the ground, chewing on the stolen flesh.

It looked up from its meal and saw Courtete staring. Its mouth opened in a silent laugh, its shoulders and belly wobbling, and it held out a long-fingered hand in invitation.

Come join me, priest. We could have fun, you and I.

And then it dropped it hand to its swollen genitals and rubbed energetically, its face glazing over in lust.

Courtete tried to drag his eyes away, but found it impossible.

The imp's movements grew more vigorous, as did the whispered words of invitation in Courtete's mind, and it was only when the imp succumbed so entirely to its lust that its eyes rolled up and it collapsed in a quivering heap on the ground that Courtete could break free from the window.

The friar took a moment to steady his mind and own physical trembling before he rejoined Planissole and the villagers.

"Bishop Fournier sent me here to help you," Courtete whispered, then cleared his throat and managed to speak more strongly. "He will spare no effort to contain this evil, and then to drive it back."

"I *have* tried everything!" Planissole said. "Every prayer that has ever been—"

"Hush, my son," Courtete said. "There is yet one more thing we can do—"

"No!" Planissole cried, and the villagers shifted and mumbled. "No!"

"My son, I am sorry, but I must. I have *seen* what . . . what scurries outside. At first light I will send a man with a letter for Bishop Fournier. He will send Maury . . . and his pack."

"No," Planissole said yet again, but his voice was very quiet now and his eyes resigned. "Is there no other way?"

"Evil is rampant," Courtete said, "and it must be driven back by the strongest of means."

The church was spacious, and there was bedding room for all the villagers, but bedding itself was at a premium, and Courtete shared Planissole's blankets behind the altar. Although both blankets and Planissole were warm, and Courtete's limbs and eyes weary from the journey to Gebetz, the scrapings on the roof and the scratchings at the windows and doors kept the friar awake with black memories of the imp's energetic hand.

Neither could Planissole sleep. "I have heard of Maury," he whispered, feeling Courtete fidget under the blanket.

"You have not seen him, or them?"

"No. I was educated much farther north, and took my orders at the great cathedral of Notre Dame."

"Ah, you are of the Parisian Planissole family, then?" No wonder the priest spoke so well! Courtete wondered what one of the aristocratic Planissoles was doing in this God-forsaken parish.

"Yes. I . . . "

Courtete's mouth thinned. A sin, then. No doubt the anonymity of the night would prompt Planissole to confess to whatever had condemned him to Gebetz, and Courtete did not know that he was in a mood to listen to a sinner's babbling.

"I became affectionate towards another novice, Father."

Courtete took a horrified breath, for the lust of one man for another was among the most appalling of sins. How was it that one man could lay the hands of lust upon another man? And force himself into another man's body? Unasked, repulsive images filled Courtete's mind, and he drew himself as far away from Planissole's body as he could. "No doubt the bishop found you rutting beneath the kitchen stairs."

"May God forgive my lusting," Planissole whispered.

Courtete wished he had chosen to spend the dark hours on his knees before the altar, and not behind it twisted in a blanket with Planissole. "In forty-five temptation-ridden years I have befouled neither my body nor my vows of chastity, Planissole," he said. "God will exact penance as he chooses, you may be sure of that."

Courtete hesitated, then spoke again, his hatred of sodomites forcing the words from his mouth. "Considering your own sin, Planissole, I find it hard to believe you regard Maury with such abhorrence."

Planissole rolled away and stood up. "I have loved my fellow man," he said quietly, "not coupled with one of the hound-bitches of Hell."

And he walked away into the darkness.

The next day Courtete sent the fittest of the village men down the mountain with a message for Bishop Fournier.

It took five days for Maury to arrive. In those five days the situation at Gebetz slid from the desperate to the abysmal. No-one now dared leave the precincts of sanctified ground; the entire population of the village, as well those transients who had sought shelter with them, was confined to the church, churchyard and adjoining graveyard. Beyond these boundaries blackened and blistered imps scurried, even during daylight hours. The legions of the dead blocked the streets, choking the gutters with their rotting effusions. The tumults of Hell wailed up through the great rents in the earth which now reached almost to the church itself, and at night immense gouts of fire speared into the night.

Evil reigned.

It would take the infernal to combat this depth of wickedness, thought Courtete as he stood in the churchyard looking down into the village. Prayers to God were useless in the face of this onslaught.

Planissole joined Courtete silently, and the friar glanced at him. Had Planissole's sin attracted this evil? But surely not even the most lascivious of sodomies could attract *this* much horror . . . could it?

Courtete returned his gaze to the streets, watching as a horned and turtle-backed demon seized a skeletal wraith and forced it to the ground for a momentary and brutal rape. Both creatures scuttled into the shadows as soon as it was done, but the vision had spread a stain across Courtete's mind and soul, and he wondered if even Maury could remove it.

Or if, perchance, he would add to it.

How *could* a man couple with a creature as foul as that imp had been?

There was a commotion in the street, and Courtete's gaze sharpened. The horned demon, so recently the aggressor, was now jumping from shadow to shadow, screaming as if God himself was after him.

"Oh Lord save us!" Planissole cried, and grabbed Courtete's sleeve. "Look!"

A creature the size of a large calf was bounding down the street. It was horned and bearded, and great yellow fangs hung from its gaping jaws. It had the paws of a dog, the tail of a lion, and the ears of a donkey, but its twisted and grotesque naked body was horrifyingly human-like.

It was female, for thin breasts swung almost to the ground.

With a shriek the she-thing pounced on the demon, pinning it to the ground, and tearing its head off with a single snap of her jaws.

Then she raised her head and stared at the two priests. She half snarled, half laughed, and bounded back into the village, looking to feed once again.

Another appeared momentarily in the doorway of the village tavern, a male-thing this time, his snakelike-head buried in the belly of a yellow-scaled sprite, his talons scrabbling at the wood doorposts, his body—as horribly human-like as the last— writhing in an agony of satisfaction.

The sprite whimpered, and dissolved, and its killer tipped back his head and howled.

Abruptly Planissole turned to one side, doubled over, and vomited. He coughed, and then straightened, wiping his mouth with the back of one hand.

"Maury's get," he said tonelessly.

"Aye," Courtete said. "The gargoyles."

As his gargoyles chased demons in and out of the houses and snapped at the heads of imps peering over the edges of chasms, Maury himself scampered down the street towards the church, apparently unconcerned about the hellish battles surrounding him. He was a twisted, wizened old man who leaned heavily on a staff, but he had merry brown eyes and a mouth almost permanently gaping in a scraggle-toothed grin.

Maury found much in life to amuse him.

He stopped before the two priests, and peered at them. "Fournier said you had a plague of evil," he said. "But I had not thought you would lay such a good table for my pets."

"Is it done?" Planissole asked.

Maury howled with laughter. "Done? *Done?* good Father? It will take a week at least to 'do' this village. But what have *you* done to attract such wretchedness? Eh? Depravity this dark does not congregate for no reason."

Again Courtete's mind filled with the memory of the imp tugging gleefully at its genitals, and to his horror the friar realised that it roused in him more than just disgust. Appalled, Courtete lost his equilibrium.

"And of depravity you would know much, wouldn't you, Maury?" he said.

Dismayed and frightened by Courtete's attack—had not the friar invited Maury himself?—Planissole laid a restraining hand on Courtete's arm, but the friar paid it no heed. "For have you not an *intimate* acquaintance with depravity?"

Maury's grin faded, and he snapped his fingers. From the window of the nearest house a gargoyle leaped to the ground and scurried over, fawning at his feet. Maury scratched the man-thing's head, but did not take his eyes from Courtete, and he understood many things.

"They are my beloveds, priest, and they will save you and yours! Do not think to condemn what you yourself—"

"Your sons and daughters do you proud," Planissole interrupted, stumbling over his words in his haste to soothe, "and for their service we may forgive the sin of their mother."

Maury's grin slowly stretched out across his face again as he looked at Planissole. "The sin of their mother, priest? She was no sin to me. She kept me warm at night, and she did not overburden me with useless chatter. And," he switched his eyes back to Courtete, "she were more willing than any *woman*, more accommodating than any *wife*, and the litters she has dropped have proved more useful to true believers of God than any *priest!*

"Besides," Maury's voice dropped to a conspiratorial level, holding Courtete's eyes, "*someone* had to couple with her, and I volunteered to save good priests the embarrassment!"

He ran an over-plump and moist tongue slowly around his lips, as if remembering his nights of abandon, and one hand scratched absently at his crotch.

Courtete's face flamed.

Maury chuckled. "Keep the villagers within the church, priests. I can keep my pets from disturbing them there."

"But—" Courtete began.

"They'll hunt down *any* evil, friar. Including the evil that these good souls harbour within them. Can you claim that any here are free of sin, free of evil? Are they not all sons of Adam and daughters of Eve?"

Maury paused, then whispered, "Are *you* not a son of Eve, friar?"

Courtete dropped his eyes and did not reply.

"And while you huddle within the church, good priests, think about what attracted this evil to Gebetz. See how these chasms reach for the church. Something here is as a beacon to it. Find it. Destroy it."

And with that he was gone.

Back to his misbegotten children.

For two days and nights Maury led them in an ecstatic hunt through the village and its enveloping clouds of sulphurous gasses, hunting out the demons, imps and sprites that continually spilled out from the rents in the earth. During that time Planissole kept his flock within the church, only allowing people out four by four to use the hastily dug communal privy pit under the alder by the graveyard. During the day the villagers huddled as close to the altar as they could get, speaking in whispers, their round, fearful eyes drifting to the bolted doors every so often.

At night they were silent, and slept in protective heaps that made Courtete shake his head and mutter prayers over lest individuals' lusts overcame their need for salvation.

Who knew what wanton communion took place among those twisted bodies?

The five or six shepherds sat by themselves several paces to the west of the altar, and the lone pilgrim, the bravest of all of them, spent his days wandering the church, studying the fine carvings and inscriptions that littered the walls.

Courtete found himself curious about the man, and yet in that curiosity, unnerved by the man's lack of perceptible fear.

At dusk of the third day after Maury's arrival, Courtete wandered over to the pilgrim as he stood by a narrow window in the eastern transept. The window was of rose glass held in lead, but even so Courtete could see the occasional dark shapes cavort outside—whether demons, imps or gargoyles, or even possibly Maury, Courtete did not know.

"Are you not afraid?" he asked the pilgrim.

The pilgrim slowly turned his eyes towards Courtete.

They were the most vivid blue Courtete had ever seen in a man.

"Afraid? In God's house? No, good friar. We are all safe within these walls."

There was a faint thump and then a scrabbling on the roof, but both men ignored it.

"Your faith is strong and lively," Courtete said, and watched the man smile cynically. "May I ask your name, and your origin?"

"My name is Malak. I come from the east, and I travel west."

Courtete opened his mouth to ask for more specifics, but was halted by the expression in Malak's eyes. The man had no desire to be further interrogated, and Courtete wondered what he had to hide.

And what an usual name! It jarred at something in Courtete's mind, but he could not place it.

"Have you seen the gargoyles before?" he asked. There were several cathedral packs in the east and north of France, and some in the German princedoms and northern Italian states, but if Malak had come from yet further east, this might be the first time he'd encountered them.

"Not this close," Malak said, and he tightened his cloak about him.

Courtete raised his eyebrows. He *was* afraid, then! "They are unsettling creatures," he prompted.

"I find it strange," Malak said softly, "that men of God fight evil with creatures that are birthed of evil and abomination."

The rooftop scrabbling came again, but more distant now.

"Good sometimes fails to—"

"Which Pope was it," Malak said, now facing Courtete again, "that decided that a mating between a man and a hound-bitch of Hell would produce a creature capable of fighting back the vilest of infamies, the darkest of Lucifer's creatures?"

"I don't know who—"

"And what kind of man *willingly* consents to plant his seed in a creature so hideous I find it difficult to imagine he could even contemplate the act of generation, let alone perform it."

There was a horribly uncomfortable quiet as each man stared at the other, each knowing the other's mind was consumed by visions of the loathsome coupling.

"Some men have a taste for such things," Courtete said and, despite himself, glanced out the rose-coloured glass as if he might again spot the imp engaged in its infernal fondling.

Malak laughed softly, as if he could read Courtete's innermost fears. "And where," he said so softly Courtete had to lean closer to hear him, "does the Church find the hound-bitches of Hell for men to couple with in the first instance?"

Courtete was silent a long time before he finally, reluctantly, replied. "In some places on God's earth the borderlands between this world and the Hellish regions under Lucifer's sway are narrow indeed. Sometimes it is possible to capture one of the Prince of Darkness' hounds."

"Aye," Malak said, "in some places the borders between this world and Hell *are* almost indefinable, indeed." He paused. "*Have* you taken a good look down those chasms outside, my friend? Do you *want* to? Might you see something down there you might *desire?*"

And with that he was gone.

Appalled that Malek could so accuse him, Courtete would have gone after the pilgrim, but just as he took his first step a horrible wailing rose from outside.

"Oh! Oh! Oh, my pretty! Oh my lovely! What do you there! Come down! Come down!"

Courtete opened the door, Planissole at his shoulder, to see Maury standing several yards away, staring at the roof. The pack of gargoyles sat yet further distant, under the low hanging eaves of a nearby house.

They were ignoring the imps that peeked at them from a nearby window, looking instead between Maury and the church roof.

"Something is wrong," Courtete murmured, and eased out the door. Planissole checked that the villagers were safely grouped about the altar, then followed, closing the door behind him.

The two priests moved to Maury, then followed his gaze upwards.

There was a gargoyle precariously balanced on the spine of the steep roof, the remains of a long-snouted imp under its claws.

It didn't look happy.

It whined, and twisted about slightly, scrabbling with its feet as it almost overbalanced. From where it sat, there was at least a twenty-pace drop.

Maury wailed.

"What is the gargoyle doing up there?" Courtete asked.

Maury twisted his hands to and fro. "She chased the imp up there . . . up *that!*"

He pointed to a rough ladder that leaned against the wall of the nave, near where it angled out into the eastern transept.

"*Who put that there?*" he shouted, and turned to Planissole, his face twisting in fury.

Planissole backed away a step. "Several weeks ago one of the villagers was engaged in relaying the slate of the roof. When the evil gathered, and everyone fled inside the church, he must have left the ladder there. But I don't understand why—"

"They *loathe* heights!" Maury said, now looking back to his gargoyle. She was still now, tense. "What if she falls?"

Planissole looked at Courtete, but the friar's face was working with what was probably disgust as he stared at the she-creature on the roof, and so the young priest gathered his courage and addressed the gargoyle keeper. "Maury, surely you can tempt her down? Speak to her soft words of reassurance? If she climbed the ladder in the first place, then—"

"What if she falls?" Maury wailed again. "How could I bear to lose her?"

And without further ado he hurried over to the ladder and began to climb it himself. "My lovely," he called, his voice soothing. "My beautiful . . . come here to me . . . come . . . yes, my pet, yes . . . come . . . "

Maury reached the top of the ladder and held out his hands to the gargoyle. "Come, my pretty, come!"

The gargoyle, reassured by the closeness of her father, slowly inched her way down the roof.

"Maury!" Planissole called. "Be careful! That ladder is—"

The gargoyle's paws slipped in the slimy residual muck of the imp. She screamed, twisted, fell on her flank, and began to slide down the roof.

Straight towards Maury.

He leaned yet further forward, thinking to break her fall with his arms, but the gargoyle was large, as heavy as a mastiff, and when she crashed into him the ladder tipped back and both Maury and the gargoyle sailed into space.

The ladder teetered, then slapped back to rest against the high guttering.

Courtete and Planissole stared, appalled. It seemed to them that the twisted forms of the gargoyle and Maury hung in space for several heartbeats, then both crashed the fifteen paces to the ground.

They landed in thick mud. There was a momentary stillness, then movement as the gargoyle struggled to her feet and limped away a few feet.

Planissole took one step forward, but Courtete grabbed his arm and hauled him back.

"Maury's dead!" he hissed. "See how still his form lies?"

"But—"

"We've got to get back inside. But move slowly, Planissole. Slowly."

"But we've got to see if—"

"By the Holy Virgin, Planissole! Maury's *dead!* Don't you understand? He was the *only* one who could control those gargoyles!"

Planissole's eyes slid towards the pack of gargoyles by the house. They were shifting anxiously, their eyes moving between the body of Maury and the two priests.

One of them lifted its head towards the priests, and snarled.

Planissole took a step back, then one more, then turned and ran. Courtete cursed, and bolted after him. Behind him he heard the pack of gargoyles raise their voices in a shrieking clamour.

"*Lord save me!*" he screamed and, now only a breath behind Planissole, ducked inside the church, slamming the door behind him.

Planissole threw down the heavy bolt. "We're safe!"

"We're *trapped!*" Courtete said. "What is to prevent those gargoyles attacking us now?'

"But we are not the evil."

Suddenly there was a scream outside, and something heavy thundered against the door.

Planissole leapt back, his hand fumbling at his cross.

A murmuring rose among the villagers, still grouped about the altar, then one cried out as a shadow flashed across one of the windows.

There was a howling outside, and numerous claws scratching at the door.

"Why us?" one of the village women cried, "when the village still swarms with fiends?"

Malak, the pilgrim, strode forth from the group. His face was taut with anger, and his eyes shone very, very bright.

He stopped just before the two priests. "Do something!" he said. "You are responsible for all our safety! Was it not enough to be surrounded by the minions of Hell? Why now are we attacked by those meant to save us?"

"You would do better," Courtete said, "to go back to the villagers and employ whatever spiritual insight you have acquired as a pilgrim to lead them in a prayer of salvation. Planissole and I will join you shortly."

Malak stared at him, then wheeled about and rejoined the villagers. He shot Courtete and Planissole a dark look, then laid his hand on the shoulder of a man and lowered his head in prayer.

The growlings and scratchings outside grew worse, more frantic. A dreadful musty odour penetrated the door; it reminded Courtete of the smell of desiccated corpses in cathedral tombs.

"Why hunt *us?*" Planissole cried.

Courtete stepped close to Planissole, and spoke quietly. "Listen to me. We are all sinners, all born of Eve. We all harbour evil within. Even you, Planissole, have freely confessed to . . . sordidness."

Planissole flinched, but spoke with angry voice. "Do you say there is no hope? Should we open the door and let the gargoyles feed at will?"

"*Listen* to me! Maury said that something acted as a beacon to attract this evil to Gebetz. *What*, Planissole? What is there in this village that would attract this much evil?"

Planissole was silent.

"If we can find this evil, and turn the gargoyles' minds to it, then we may yet be saved. What, Planissole? What?"

The young man shook his head. "What village sin could attract this much retribution? There has been no great sin committed here. No murders. No invocations to the Prince of Darkness. Nothing but the daily sins of ordinary men and women."

"No incest? How can you know what goes on in the crowded beds of the village houses? I know peasants." Courtete's voice thickened with disgust. "Entire families share the one precious bed. Fathers huddle with daughters, mothers with sons. Flesh is weak, Planissole, and temptation strong. Who knows what happens when a man stretches out his hand in the night and encounters the breast of his daughter, a woman the manhood of her son. No doubt—"

"Your mind is consumed with the temptations of the flesh, is it not, Courtete?" Planissole said flatly. "You accuse all around you of impurity, yet of what do *you* dream at night? The saints? Or of the humping blankets of peasant beds? Do you yearn to lift the corners of those blankets to watch, Courtete? *Do* you?"

Planissole turned away momentarily, taking a deep breath to calm his anger. What is the greater sin, he thought. The sin of the flesh committed yet confessed, or the sins of the mind not admitted? "My parishioners sin no more than those in Arques, Courtete, no more than those in Toulouse or Orleons or Paris itself. I have no reason to put forward for this all-consuming evil that has attacked *us*."

"What? Are you sure that *you* have not sullied the innocence of a shepherd boy, Planissole? Are you *certain* you have not engaged in an 'affection' with one of those young dark-eyed boys? Or were the sheep more compliant, perhaps?"

Planissole grabbed the front of Courtete's robe. "I do not think it *me* lusting for the sheep, Brother Courtete!"

Courtete blanched, and trembled. "Lucifer himself must be guiding our tongues, Planissole. Fighting between ourselves will not aid us, nor the villagers. My son, I suggest we lead these poor souls in prayer, and hope that the Lord hears our entreaties."

Planissole jerked his head in assent—and some residual disgust—and let go Courtete's robe. "You speak sense, Brother. 'Tis the Lord God only who can forgive sin."

He walked over to the villagers, and gathered them for prayer. Courtete joined him, and together they led the assembly in a prayer for salvation even as the gargoyles renewed their attack on the church doors.

"From those that reareth wars, from those that maketh tempests, from those that maketh debate between neighbours and manslaughter therewith, from those that stoketh fires, and those that bloweth down houses, steeples and trees—"

"*Free and defend us, O Lord!*"

"From the stratagems and snares of the devil—"

"*Free and defend us, O Lord!*"

"From the onslaught of malignant fiends—"

"*Free and defend us, O Lord!*"

"From ourselves—"

"*Free and defend us, O Lord!*"

As the response faded, Courtete opened his mouth to begin a litany against hopelessness, when Malak laughed loudly.

His eyes were still angry.

"Do you think to drive back such as assaults this church with such pitiful words, priest?"

"It is all we have, my son."

Malak's mouth twisted. "It is the evil within that makes the gargoyles attack, Courtete. Perhaps *your* evil. How many of these women have you lusted after, Courtete? And how many of the boys, Planissole?"

He turned and addressed the villagers. "Perhaps we should just throw the *priests* to the gargoyles! Prayer will not save us! Well, what say you? Shall we throw those tainted creatures outside the tainted minds of these priests?"

"Be still, Malak!" Courtete roared, and at the name he spoke Planissole went white with shock. "Can you claim to be free of sin yourself?"

But Malak did not answer him. He was staring at Planissole, and his teeth bared in a cold smile.

"You know my name, do you not, priest?"

Planissole slowly sunk to his knees, his face now rigid with dread. He opened his mouth, but no sound came forth.

Courtete stared at Malek, then at Planissole. "My friend," he said gently, "what is it?"

"Malek," Planissole whispered harshly, "is an ancient word for angel."

He threw himself to the stone flagging, prostrating himself before the angel.

"Save us! Save us!"

Malek the angel stepped back and laughed. "Nay, not I!"

Courtete fought down the cold terror within—had the angel seen the visions of the imp that filled his mind?—and addressed the angel as calmly as he could. "What do you here? Why do your immortal feet tread this earth?"

"I come bearing word from God, to all sinners on earth."

"And that word is . . . ?"

"The word is being acted out about you, Courtete. Sin inundates this wasteland, and grows worse each day. The evil within, within you," the angel pointed at Courtete, "and within you," his finger stabbed towards Planissole still face down on the flagging, "and within all of you," the accusing finger swept over the huddled, frightened villagers, "has grown so great that Lucifer's legions have surged out of Hell to greet it! God's wrath increases with each imp that scampers into the light of day, and He has grown of the mind that He should abandon you to your fate."

"No!" Courtete cried, and also fell to his knees. "Say it is not so! What must we do? How can we save ourselves?"

The angel stepped forward and grabbed Courtete's hair, twisting his face up. "Are you prepared to throw yourself to the gargoyles, Courtete? Will you sacrifice yourself for these villagers as Christ sacrificed himself for mankind? And you, Planissole? Will you also let the gargoyles tear you apart as Christ endured the spear and nails for your sakes?"

Both Courtete and Planissole were silent. Then, "If it will save these good folk, then, yes, I will so offer myself," Planissole said, rising to his knees.

His voice was almost joyous.

After a momentary hesitation, Courtete also spoke. "And I."

"Then spend the night in prayer," the angel said, "in the hope that God will accept your souls. At dawn I will open those doors and you will step forth to assuage the anger of the gargoyles."

The interior of the church was shadowed, the only light cast by the flickering candles on the altar.

No-one slept.

The villagers and shepherds were now at the rear of the nave, seated stiff and frightened against the back wall, as far from the angel as they could get.

He, for his part, sat cross-legged in the very centre of the nave, staring towards where the folded rood screen revealed the altar.

There knelt the two priests, their backs to the angel, deep in prayer.

Or so it seemed.

"Something is not as it should be," Courtete murmured.

"Be joyful, brother. We will save the villagers with our deaths."

"No, no. It is not a lack of acceptance that makes me so uneasy. There is *something* not right."

Planissole decided not to reply, and the silence deepened between them.

Eventually Courtete whispered again. "If he is God's messenger, then why does he linger *here*?"

Planissole was silent.

"Should the angel not be out, spreading God's message? Is that not his mission?"

Planissole began murmuring the Pater Noster, but Courtete knew he was listening.

"Planissole, the angel is as afraid of those gargoyles as we are. He has stayed within this church because he is terrified of them!"

Planissole continued murmuring, but the words of the prayer were broken now. Faltering.

"No angel should fear a gargoyle," Courtete continued. "Not unless he . . . unless he . . . "

Planissole breathed in sharply. "Unless he is a *fallen* angel!"

"Angels can sin as much—greater!—than man! Is not Lucifer himself a fallen angel? And does not Lucifer gather to him all angels who have fallen from grace?"

"*He* is the beacon which has attracted the evil to Gebetz! Our plight worsened significantly after he arrived." Planissole paused. "Perhaps . . . perhaps Lucifer has thought to open Hell about us here so that the angel may join him. Thus the rents in the earth, the sulphurous odours!"

"Aye. Perhaps the angel thinks to escape to the nearest chasm while the gargoyles are occupied with us."

Planissole grinned in the dark. "I have an idea. One to rid us of angel, gargoyles *and* evil."

Outside the gargoyles paced back and forth, occasionally scratching at the wooden doors, occasionally howling and screaming their frustration.

They wanted the evil within.

At dawn the angel rose and walked over to the two priests still bowed in prayer. He laid a hand each on their shoulders.

"It is time."

The two men rose stiffly to their feet. Planissole looked ashen and sweaty, his eyes frightened.

"I . . . I . . . " he stumbled. "My bowels . . . I am sorry."

And he rushed towards some stairs that wound up to a store room built among the roof beams. Beneath the staircase was a small closet with a pot set up for the effluent of mortals; few now wished to venture out to the open privy under the alder.

The angel hissed in frustration.

"He is young," Courtete said, "and scared. It is to be expected."

The angel looked at Courtete. The man's face was calm and relaxed.

"You should, perhaps, exhibit more fear yourself, friar. Too soon you will be torn—" The angel stopped, then cried out in anger. "See! He thinks to escape!"

Instead of stepping inside the small closet, Planissole had leaped onto the stairs and was now climbing rapidly.

"Fool!" Courtete cried enthusiastically. "Accept your fate!"

And he sprinted towards the stairs.

The angel screamed in fury, the unearthly sound echoing about the church, and then he, too, ran for the stairs that now both priests were climbing as fast as they could.

The stairs twisted in a tight, narrow circular fashion, and when the angel reached their base all he could see was the climbing feet of Courtete high above.

Planissole was nowhere to be seen.

The angel's hands tightened into talons as he grabbed hold of the railings, and he bounded up the stairs three at a time, howling as he climbed.

His face twisted and contorted into that of a bearded demon, his back humped into grotesque lumps, and his clothes burst from him.

Courtete turned as he heard the angel step onto the platform behind him, and almost screamed.

All semblance of the man had gone. The angel had now assumed the form of a multi-armed, pot-bellied, toad-skinned creature.

It snarled, flecks of yellow foam splattering about.

Courtete swallowed, and flung his hand towards the open window. "He's climbed out onto the roof!"

The angel-demon scurried over to the window and looked out, twisting to view the slope of the roof above. "Where?" it growled.

"He . . . he . . . " Courtete found it almost impossible to force the words out. "He has climbed over the spine of the roof. Perhaps he hopes to escape down the ladder on the other side."

The angel-demon hissed, then, its claws scrabbling furiously for purchase, lifted itself out of the window and onto the roof.

Courtete heard its feet thudding as it climbed.

"*Lord save us!*" he screamed, and slammed the shutters of the window shut.

In an instant Planissole leapt out of his hiding place behind a set of hessian-wrapped bells and helped his fellow priest bolt the window closed.

"Are you sure there is no other way he can get down from the roof?" Courtete gasped.

"No! No . . . *listen!*"

Something horrible was jabbering on the roof above them. It whispered and shrieked and scampered, and the priests could hear the promise of Hell in its voice.

"Quick!" Courtete said. "We have no time to waste!"

And as fast as they had climbed the stairs, they hurried down.

Once back to the church floor they did not waste a glance at the villagers still huddled in a silent mass, but ran to the door. Courtete put his ear to the wood and listened intently.

"Nothing," he whispered. "Silence."

Then something screamed high above them, and one of the village women wailed.

Courtete and Planissole shared a look, then unbolted the door, hurriedly crossed themselves, and stepped outside.

The space before the church was empty.

There were no gargoyles to be seen.

As one both men turned towards the ladder.

It was swarming with gargoyles. Already the first was clambering onto the roof, another at its tail. As the men watched, the final gargoyle on the ground climbed onto the first rungs of the ladder.

"Sweet Jesu," Planissole whispered. "Climb! Climb!"

Above the angel-demon shrieked and gibbered. The men could hear it scrambling about agilely enough, but now four or five gargoyles were creeping their careful way towards it. Not long, and they would have it trapped.

Courtete made as if to move forward, but Planissole held him back with a cautionary hand. "Wait . . . wait . . . *now!*"

They darted forward as the final gargoyle made its way onto the roof, seized the ladder in shaking hands, and pulled it backwards until it toppled to the ground.

"Done!" Courtete yelled. "*Done!*"

The gargoyles took no notice, but the angel-demon—now clinging to the cross that rose from the centre of the roof above the nave—began to rain curses down upon them.

"May demons eviscerate you for this! May imps violate your mothers! May you be cursed to the pits of Hell for . . . *ah!*"

A gargoyle bit down on one of its arms, and then another sank its teeth deep into its belly, and another its neck.

The angel-demon screamed and tried to tear itself free, but the gargoyles tore deeper.

An arm came free, black blood spraying across the roof.

What was left of the angel-demon tried to curl into a ball to protect its belly—but it was too late, green-grey entrails already spilled about its knees, and the creature slipped in its own mess and was instantly covered by the pack of gargoyles.

The priests watched silently as the gargoyles tore the evil thing apart.

And then . . . silence.

Nothing. The gargoyles crouched to the slate, as if suddenly realising where they were. The wind dropped. No howls. No shrieks.

Planissole looked back into the village.

Houses still leaned helter skelter into great cracks in the earth, but now no sulphurous fumes rose skyward. No blackened imps' heads poked above the edges of the fissures.

Lucifer had closed the gates of Hell, his disciple destroyed.

"Praise the Lord the evil was strong enough to tempt those gargoyles to the roof," Courtete said.

One of the creatures glanced down . . . and growled.

"Praise God the evil *above* was the greater temptation," Planissole said.

Six months later Courtete returned to the village of Gebetz. The sky was lightly clouded, but sun fell on the village, and at the top of the mountain track Courtete stopped and leaned on his staff, astonished.

It seemed that this place did not know the meaning of evil, let alone be a site that had nurtured such horror only a half year earlier. Carefully tended fields spread up the mountains, and where the slope grew too steep for cropping, there flourished sweet pastures.

Within the village itself the houses had been repaired; all stood straight and even. The streets were paved, and flowers grew in window boxes.

People wandered the streets, gossiping or bargaining at the produce stalls, their eyes free of anything save laughter and good cheer.

Courtete looked to the church, and his wonder grew.

It lay swathed in sunshine amid emerald lawns. The doors were flung wide open so that God's goodness and mercy might spill down upon the village.

Crouched about the roof were the immobile shapes of the gargoyles.

Courtete slowly descended into the village, passing a few words here and there with villagers who remembered him.

When he approached the church, Planissole stepped forth and hurried down the slope to meet him.

"My friend! It is good to see you again!" he cried.

Then Planissole's face grew serious. "What did Bishop Fournier say? Was he angry?"

"Nay, Planissole. Do not fret. Fournier was naturally somewhat upset at the loss of the pack, but they were useless without Maury to control them. Tell me, do they give you any trouble?"

"None. At night we sometimes hear them move about, but mostly they crouch at the extremities of the roof, as they are now. In fact, no-one has seen or heard them move for several weeks."

"And the evil?"

"None. No evil dares approach Gebetz now the gargoyles stand sentinel upon the church roof. Even the mountain trails are clear."

Courtete raised his eyes to the roof again, thinking about what he would say to Fournier when he returned to Arques. What a God-given answer to dealing with the problem of evil *and* the perennial problem with coping with the fractious packs of gargoyles! Fournier had ordered another pack from the gargoyle breeding groves of the Black Forest—but why not simply station them on the roof of the cathedral and send their keeper packing?

After all, what God-fearing man could trust someone who *enjoyed* fornicating with a hound-bitch from Hell? Courtete shuddered, and tried unsuccessfully to force the visions of unnatural intercourse from his mind.

"One day," he said quietly to Planissole, "every church roof in Christendom shall bristle with such as these."

"And that," the younger priest replied, "should leave us to devour our sheep in complete freedom, should it not, Courtete?"

Author's Note

A truly dark tale, inspired by the medieval concept of evil and the wonderful medieval village of Montaillou. This story was selected as one of the best fantasy stories in the world for 1998 and also appears in The Year's Best Fantasy & Horror, *edited by Ellen Datlow and Terri Windling, published by St Martin's Griffin in New York.*

THE HALL OF LOST FOOTSTEPS

THE HALL OF LOST FOOTSTEPS

SARA DOUGLASS & ANGELA SLATTER

The entire valley was blanketed in an oppressive heat. Meadows and vineyards clinging to the steep slopes of the mountain shimmered under the relentless sun. The stubbled fields on the floor of the valley were barren of movement save for the humming, hovering clouds of insects over dried cattle and sheep dung. Only a few folk shuffled about in the village, and those only to seek shelter in the shade of a tree, or a doorway.

And when they did stir, they glanced over their shoulders, as if expecting the shadows of hell to chase them down.

A child cried briefly, inconsolably, in the still afternoon, and was hushed by the worried voice of its mother.

The sole thing that dared to move was the silvery stream that danced through the heart of the valley.

That . . . and *her*. The woman they all loathed, but needed. Isolde, the single, solitary individual who would be able to deflect the coming terror. Isolde. The witch.

Isolde scratched about in the herb garden with a trowel, then sat back on her heels, forearm wiping the perspiration from her forehead. Her back ached, and her temples throbbed. She knew she should be inside in the dim, cool shade, but Isolde could not bear the silence of the waiting shadows. Not today. She had known upon waking this morning that today would bring the summons . . . but to allow that knowledge to alter her routine would be to allow it to defeat her. So she had done her best to treat this day as any other. She had risen, breakfasted on the remains of yesterday's bread, and tidied her single room cottage, folding away the bed linens from the small sleeping couch. Then Isolde had tended to the chores—washing out her aprons, feeding the chickens and geese, damping down the fire until she needed to revive it for the evening's baking.

But this evening—would she still be here?

Isolde rose, grimacing and rubbed at the small of her back and then, involuntarily, glanced up to the head of the valley to where the ancient castle rose grim and hard from the mountain.

He lived there, her lord, the lord of the entire valley. The Count of Montplessier. The man who granted the villagers the use of the fields, their homes, the meadows and woodlands. The man who provided the ale and food for the post-harvest feasts, and ensured a living for the priest who nurtured the villagers' souls. In return, each of the households provided the count with a service. More than half provided men and boys to work the fields, to cut and gather the wood to heat his hall. Others, the women to bake his bread, and yet others, the girls to launder his linens.

For her cottage and acre of land, Isolde had just a very small obligation, and that only once a year. Yet she feared, eventually, that one day would cost her life.

She tore her eyes away from the castle and looked at the rows of herbs and the arbours of flowers. This garden was her only friend. It gave her many hours of pleasure and much of her food.

It also supplied a small income. Once or twice a week one of the villagers would visit—their approach always stealthy, their stay always brief—and Isolde would give them the infusions and ointments they needed for their work-worn hands and blistered feet, and the torn and strained muscles of their weary bodies. They never thanked her, but Isolde would usually wake two or three mornings later to find a dressed rabbit on her doorstep, or a basket of fruit, and sometimes even a side of bacon, if the ache had been bad enough.

Isolde shook her head. Loneliness, a constant companion, threatened to overwhelm her. She'd been loved once, but that love was long dead. Her husband—*God, she couldn't remember his features!*—had been taken by a fever, some sickness that had swept down from the mountains and carried away several of the villagers. They'd had no children, although . . . Isolde frowned, trying to remember . . . she had been pregnant once. *Hadn't she?*

She had lost it, perhaps? Those difficult first months without him . . . yes, that was it . . . the shock . . .

Ah! When each year blended seamlessly into the other, it was no wonder events and faces were lost so easily to the vagaries of memory.

Isolde turned and walked towards the small lean-to that held her gardening forks and hoes, meaning to put away the trowel, when she stopped. Her heart thumped, her eyes widened and she was suddenly terrified.

She whipped about, looking towards the track leading away from her cottage. It twisted and turned, winding between low, spreading olive trees, but Isolde could see the dust rising a half mile away, and she could hear the pounding of the hoofbeats.

And she could see, in her mind's eye, the grim determined faces of the men who rode onward—their rigid shoulders, the thin lines of their mouths, the white knuckles of the hands that clutched the reins.

The hate in their eyes. The bitter satisfaction.

Isolde closed her own eyes and moaned softly, the trowel dropping unheeded into the dry dirt. She sank slowly to her haunches, wrapping her arms about her knees, eyes now open and riveted on the small section of the track where she knew they would appear.

Another minute, no more, and they would be upon her.

They galloped straight into her garden, heedless of their mounts' trampling iron shoes.

The Count of Montplessier reined his horse to a rearing halt, so close to Isolde that dirt from its plunging hooves sprayed over her.

"I need you," he said.

She slowly rose, wiping her hands down the skirt of her dress. She stared at the count, seeing his loathing, and knowing that it grew from his need. It made him a beggar before her.

She didn't answer immediately, and he grew impatient. He was used to achieving his ends with a single word spoken, a man who expected—and got—the deference of everyone in the valley, a man who rested easy in the knowledge that homage was his by right.

But he also knew that none of that mattered when it came to this woman.

"*I need you*," he said again.

Isolde glanced behind him. He had an escort of six men, but no spare horses.

He needed her, but she would have to walk.

She looked back at him, noting the deep lines under his eyes and running from nose to mouth. Sadness and sleeplessness had made him old before his time.

"Have they sounded?" she asked.

"Aye," he said. "This past week. You know that."

She sighed, and dropped her eyes from his face. "I had hoped—"

"I hope every year," he said, voice harsh, "but every year they return."

"You should have called me sooner."

But he had not, and Isolde knew why. He would have tried without her, tried to reason with the lost creature that trampled through his castle, and every night that he delayed the weeping would have grown stronger and the footsteps louder. Every year he tried and every year he failed . . . this year was no exception.

"It wants you," he said.

She sighed once more. "I will come," she said, and the count nodded, and swung his horse's head back down the track.

When they got to the castle it was mid-afternoon, and so hot that Isolde felt as if she might faint. She'd walked, as she'd known she must, the entire way at the head of the horsemen hearing every muffled hoofbeat behind her, feeling the constant stare of every man on her back.

Isolde the witch, off to practice her sorcery.

Sorcery? Isolde leaned against the rising wall of the outer keep, fighting tears. "You have no time for rest," yelled the count from behind her. "Walk on."

Isolde bit back a retort, almost hating him. *No wonder that lost thing could not rest!*

She revived a little when she walked under the archway into the castle courtyard, deep in cool shadow.

It was also crowded.

Isolde stopped, looking about. The entire population of the castle—the cooks, grooms, soldiers, guards, boys, maids, valets, pages, housemen—were waiting.

Waiting for her . . . waiting for her to make it safe to go back inside.

The count halted his horse beside Isolde, and swung down. He put his hand on her elbow, and she was surprised by the gentleness of his touch.

"I'm thirsty," she murmured.

"Of course." The count gestured, and a servant approached with a pitcher and cup. Isolde thanked the man softly then drank, as grateful for the liquid as she was for the delay it bought her.

He departed, not acknowledging her thanks.

The count's fingers tightened on her again, tenderness flown. Isolde took a deep breath, then walked forward. The count's hand drop away as she did so.

He would come no further.

High on its perch on the mountain crag, the castle was dominating, but not overly large. There was the great hall, built many generations earlier by one of the count's ancestors, the service rooms—kitchen, pantries, buttery, laundries, storerooms and the servants' quarters—that filled the floor beneath the hall and a service wing that extended between the hall and the stable complex. The count's private apartments filled a small wing that ran off the back of the very hall.

And it was the hall itself that was the problem.

Or, rather, where the problem resided.

Isolde entered slowly, hearing the arched doors close softly behind her. She was beyond fear now, and settled into resignation. Here she was again . . . and here *it* was again, waiting for her, as it did every year.

She stopped, looking about her. The stone hall extended east-west for almost one hundred paces. Its vaulted ceiling reached sixty paces high—Isolde could only imagine the number of stonemasons who had lost their lives trying to put that in—and a row of clear-paned windows, each ten paces high and arched to mirror the shape of the doors, ran down the northern wall, a little below waist height.

As she ever did, Isolde walked over and stared out the closest window. The view was spectacular—the entire valley spread out before her—but Isolde was not drawn by the view. Instead, she was drawn by the tragedy that still lingered . . . here, by the fourth window along.

Here the count's wife had rested on the narrow windowsill. Here the count's wife had leaned, made breathless by the beauty of the scenery.

Here she had fallen to her death, leaning too far and toppling out an insecurely fastened window into the void below.

Villagers whispered said her body was still down there, somewhere deep within a fissure in the mountain rock.

As lost to human aid as if she lay in the depths of the ocean.

There was a breath of movement behind Isolde, the faint scraping of a footstep.

She froze, still at the window, back stiff, eyes staring sightlessly into the space beyond the glass.

Again, the faint shuffle of a footfall.

Isolde abruptly moved, scrambled away from the window, sure that if she stayed, she too would be pitched to her death.

She could feel it now, the icy wind of her passing as she plunged into the mountain chasm!

Isolde drew in a deep breath, bringing her fear under control. These were memories only, and not hers. The memories of that tragic woman . . . and the child she carried.

The child who now haunted this place.

Isolde walked slowly into the centre of the hall. Every year in late summer the child's footsteps echoed along the timber flooring. Always starting softly, late one night perhaps, a brief scattering of faint footfalls. But as the days went by, and the valley slid deeper into the grip of the unnatural heat the child's presence brought with it, the footsteps grew bolder, angrier, more *demanding*.

And every year, the count waited, between a week to ten days before he capitulated and finally sent for Isolde.

Isolde frowned, trying to remember the first year of the sending. His wife had fallen to her death ten years ago, and so Isolde had been coming here for nine years.

Why her? Why had he asked for her? How had the child communicated its need for her?

Isolde frowned, shaking her head. Why couldn't she remember? Why did everything seem so confused?

Why couldn't she remember her husband's face? Or the features of the count's wife, for that matter?

Isolde had lived all her life in this valley, hadn't she? Surely she had seen the woman on countless occasions . . . hadn't she?

Why couldn't she remember? Her name . . . her name was . . .

"I'm getting old," she murmured, angry with her failing memory, with this sudden tormenting obsession.

Every year she walked into this hall, every year she walked over to the window and stared out . . . and every year she tried to remember . . . *something*.

Then Isolde jumped, her heart racing. Footsteps echoed, the footsteps of a small child, racing up and down the chamber's length. Playing, she would say if she didn't know better. She twisted around, but saw nothing, as every year she saw nothing.

"There, there," Isolde whispered, slowly turning as she looked about the room. "Don't fret, don't fret . . . "

The padding slowed, and Isolde's heart thudded the harder as she heard them approach her.

Sometimes they did this, slowly circling her, stalking her, with such a heavy malevolence that Isolde knew, *knew* that one day it would not be comforted into submission.

The footsteps stopped, and Isolde could sense the child standing some few paces away.

She swallowed. "Don't fret," she whispered, and cried out, terrified, as she felt the presence hurtle towards her.

She fell to the floor. "No!"

Nothing, save the heaving of her own breath. She raised herself slowly. "What do you want?" she whispered. "What?"

Nothing.

Then the faint patter of footsteps, running away from her now.

Towards the window.

The catch screeched, then lifted, and very slowly, painfully slowly, the window swung out into the void.

A coldness consumed Isolde. "No!"

The footsteps started back towards her. Heavy, purposeful.

What did it want? For her to jump out? Why? Vengeance? Anger that its mother's carelessness had killed it, and so it would now take someone else's life?

Is that all it had wanted all these years?

Isolde, still sitting on the floor, began to inch towards the back wall, as far from the window as she could get. "No," she said, as firmly as she could. "No."

The footsteps grew more menacing. They were very close to her now, and even though Isolde could not *see* the child, she could sense it almost as if it were a weight, a thickening in the air, slowly approaching.

The window shifted in an errant breeze, banging gently against its frame before swinging out again.

The footsteps, very deliberately, came yet closer.

"I have done you no wrong," Isolde said. "What good can come of my death?"

The footsteps paused briefly, then began their slow, purposeful treading again.

Isolde scrambled yet further away, faster now, her eyes darting to the closed door. What had she done last year? What?

Was she to be the sacrifice? Is this what the village had decided?

Isolde whimpered, then managed to get to her feet. Again she looked at the door. A tune echoed in her mind. A lullaby.

Something tugged at her skirt.

Isolde cried out, backing away a few paces, pulling her skirt free of ghostly hands.

"Leave me be, child," she said as calmly as she could. "Be at peace." She began to hum, trying to keep her voice rich and warm, but her fear was so strong that the sound was jerky, and the tune disjointed.

Go away! She thought. *Just go away!*

The child grabbed at her skirt again, and this time it did not let go.

Isolde stopped humming. She took her skirt in both hands and tugged, but she could not dislodge the child's grip.

Her eyes flew to the window.

It now stood wide open.

Isolde sobbed, once, deep, then cried out, "No! No! No!"

The eldritch grip tightened, and with deadly strength it dragged her towards the window. She fell.

Isolde screamed for the count, screamed for aid, but none came. Her entire existence seemed as if it were wrapped in an icy nothingness, as if she had been pulled across the boundary between her world and the cold child's.

The footsteps echoed louder, and with each step the child's strength grew, so that within moments Isolde found herself being dragged towards to the window with such speed that at every heavy footfall her head and shoulders thudded painfully against the floor. She twisted about, trying to snag her fingers at something—at *anything*—but it was no use. It seemed as if ten strong men had her, hauling her towards the gaping window . . .

Isolde screamed, twisting and rolling, and then she slammed into the wall below the window with such force that for a few, painful moments she could not draw air at all.

The child's grip had vanished. The hall was silent.

Isolde managed to get her breath, then she slowly rose to her knees. Her entire body was shaking.

A breeze from the window ruffled her hair, and she cringed, crying out involuntarily.

Yet again she glanced at the door.

A footfall sounded directly before her, as if blocking any hope of escape . . . and then she felt a hand, a small, plump hand, grasp at her wrist. Its touch was warm, its flesh very slightly moist.

It tugged gently, urging her to rise.

She resisted, but the child did not let go, nor did it increase the strength of its grip. It tugged again, almost kindly.

Then, stunningly, Isolde thought she heard the sound of soft weeping.

Very slowly, her eyes wide and staring, Isolde raised her free hand to the window sill and lifted herself to her feet.

She glanced to her left where gaped the window, and swayed in horror at the sight of the plunging void beyond.

The child tugged at her other wrist, pulling her centre of balance away from danger.

Isolde stared down at the wrist held in the child's invisible grip, almost unable to believe what it had done. A simple movement, a flick, and, as unbalanced as she was, it could have toppled her out of the window.

"What do you want?" she whispered.

There was no reply, save a very slight increase of pressure about her wrist.

Isolde leaned against the windowsill, not daring to look outside. She was trembling so badly she thought that she would probably fall anyway.

The child's grip suddenly tightened again . . . and Isolde felt the child pull itself into her lap. There it sat, small and invisible, trembling as if it were afraid. Still shaking, Isolde slid her free arm about the child, and felt it snuggle into her.

It whimpered, a child trying to wake from a nightmare.

Isolde, incredulous, tightened her hold the thing she could not see, cradling it close, then reached out with one hand, grasped the lower edge of the window, and swung it closed.

The latch clicked.

"Isolde!"

She blinked, surprised by the fear in the voice, and looked up.

The hall was different, clothed in a cooler light, and trestle tables and chairs stood about, as if a meal had just been concluded. A man was striding towards her . . . it was the count, but a younger and merrier man than she knew.

Isolde sprang to her feet, almost losing her balance at the strange heaviness of her body, and wondering if, somehow, she had fallen alseep by the window. Excuses sprang to her lips, but the count gave her no time to mouth them. He leaned down, and took her shoulders in his hands. Then, stunningly, he kissed her.

"My dear," he said, his eyes both merry and worried at the same time, "how many times have I told you to be careful by the windows? One day a latch will give way and you shall tumble out."

She wrinkled her brow, confused, and then felt a movement within her as if . . . as if of a child. She looked down, and saw that she was swollen with child.

THE
SILENCE
OF THE
DYING

THE SILENCE OF THE DYING

SARA DOUGLASS

Many years ago I did an hour long interview on Adelaide radio (with Jeremy Cordeaux, I think, but my memory may be wrong). The interview was supposed to promote one of my recent publications, but for some reason we quickly strayed onto the subject of death and dying, and there we stayed for the entire hour. I proposed that as a society we have lost all ability to die well. Unlike pre-industrial western society, modern western society is ill at ease with death, we are not taught how to die, and very few people are comfortable around death or the dying. There is a great silence about the subject, and a great silence imposed on the dying. During the programme a Catholic priest called in to agree with the premise (the first and last time a Catholic priest and I have ever agreed on anything) that modern society cannot deal with death. We just have no idea. We are terrified of it. We ignore it and we ignore the dying.

Today I'd like to take that conversation a little further, discuss modern discomfort with death, and discuss the silence that modern western society imposes on the dying. Recently I've had it hammered home on a couple of occasions how much the dying are supposed to keep silent, that "dying well" in today's society means keeping your mouth firmly closed and, preferably, behind closed doors.

Never shall a complaint pass your lips. How many times have we all heard that praise sung of the dying and recently departed, "They never complained"?

Death in pre-industrial society was a raucous and social event. There was much hair-tearing, shrieking and breast beating, and that was just among the onlookers. Who can forget the peripatetic late-medieval Margery Kempe who shrieked and wailed so exuberantly she was in demand at all the death beds she happened across? Suffering, if not quite celebrated, was at least something to which everyone could relate, and with which everyone was at ease. People were comfortable with death and with the dying. Death was not shunted away out of sight. Grief was not subdued. Emotions were not repressed. If someone was in pain or feeling a bit grim or was frightened, they were allowed to express those feelings. Unless they died suddenly, most people died amid familiar company and in their own homes amid familiar surroundings. Children were trained in the art and craft of dying well from an early age (by being present at community death beds). Death and dying was familiar, and its journey's milestones well marked and recognisable. People prepared from an early age to die, they were always prepared, for none knew when death would strike.

Not any more. Now we ignore death. We shunt it away. Children are protected from it (and adults wish they could be protected from it). The dying are often not allowed to express what they are really feeling, but are expected (by many pressures) to be positive, bright and cheerful as "this will make them feel better" (actually, it doesn't make the dying feel better at all, it just makes them feel worse, but it does make their dying more bearable for those who have to be with them).

When it comes to death and dying, we impose a dreadful silence on the dying lest they discomfort the living too greatly.

I have done no study as to when the change took place, but it must have been about or just before the Industrial Revolution—perhaps with the mass movement into the cities and the subsequent destruction of traditional communities and community ties, perhaps with the rise of the modern medical profession who demanded to control every aspect of illness, perhaps with the loosening grip of religion on people's lives during the Enlightenment.

Certainly by the nineteenth century silence and restraint had overtaken the dying. The Victorian ideal was of the dying suffering sweetly and stoically and silently (we've all read the novels, we've all seen the paintings). Those who didn't die sweetly and stoically and silently but who bayed their distress to the moon generally ended badly by dropping their candle on their flammable nightgown, and then expiring nastily in the subsequent conflagration which took out the east tower of whatever gothic mansion they inhabited. The lingering commotion and the smouldering ruins always disturbed everyone's breakfast the next morning. There was much tsk-tsk-tsk-ing over the marmalade.

By the mid-nineteenth century, if not earlier, the lesson was clearly implanted in our society's collective subconscious.

Death should be silent. Confined. Stoic.

Sweet, stoic and silent was the way to go. (Again I remind you that a sweet, stoic and silent death is still praised innumerable times in today's society; by the time we have reached early adulthood we have all heard it many, many times over.) The one exception is the terminally ill child. Terminally ill children are uncritisable saints. The terminally ill adult is simply tedious (particularly if they try to express their fears).

All this silence and stoicism scares the hell out of me.

In that radio interview many years ago I spoke as a historian. Today I speak as one among the dying. Two years ago I was diagnosed with cancer. Six months ago it came back. It is going to kill me at some stage. Now everyone wants a date, an expected life span, an answer to the "how long have you got?" question. I don't know. I'm sorry to be inconvenient. I am not in danger of imminent demise, but I will not live very long. So now I discuss this entire "how we treat the dying" with uncomfortable personal experience.

Now, with death lurking somewhere in the house, I have begun to notice death all about me. I resent every celebrity who "has lost their long battle with cancer". Oh God, what a cliché. Can no one think of anything better? It isn't anything so noble as a "battle" gallantly lost, I am afraid. It is just a brutal, frustrating, grinding, painful, demoralising, terrifying deterioration that is generally accomplished amid great isolation.

Let me discuss chronic illness for a moment. As a society we don't tolerate it very well. Our collective attention span for someone who is ill lasts about two weeks. After that they're on their own. From my own experience and talking to others with bad cancer or chronic illness, I've noticed a terrible trend. After a while, and only a relatively short while, people grow bored with you not getting any better and just drift off. Phone calls stop. Visits stop. Emails stop. People drop you off their Facebook news feed. Eyes glaze when you say you are still not feeling well. Who needs perpetual bad news?

This is an all too often common experience. I described it once to a psychologist, thinking myself very witty, as having all the lights in the house turned off one by one until you were in one dark room all alone; she said everyone described it like that. People withdraw, emotionally and physically. You suddenly find a great and cold space about you where once there was support. For me there has been a single person who has made the effort to keep in daily contact with me, to see how I am, how I am feeling, and listen uncomplainingly to my whining. She has been my lifeline. She also suffers from terrible cancer and its aftermath, and has endured the same distancing of her friends.

The end result is, of course, that the sick simply stop telling people how bad they feel. They repress all their physical and emotional pain, because they've got the message loud and clear.

People also don't know how to help the sick and dying. I remember a year or so ago, on a popular Australian forum, there was a huge thread generated on how to help a member who was undergoing massive and life-changing surgery that would incapacitate her for months. People asked what they could do. I suggested that if one among them, or many taking it in turns, could promise this woman two hours of their time every week or fortnight for the next few months then that would help tremendously. In this two hours they could clean, run errands, hang out the washing, whatever. And they had to do all this while not once complaining about how busy their own lives were, or how bad their back was, or how many problems they had to cope with in life. Just two hours a fortnight, with no emotional-guilt strings attached. Whatever she wanted or needed. Freely given.

Bliss for the incapacitated or chronically ill.

But that was too difficult. Instead the poor woman was buried under a mountain of soft toys, dressing gowns, bath salts and bombs, daintily embroidered hankies, a forest's worth of Hallmark cards, chocolates and flowers and exhortations that everyone was "thinking of her".

None of which helped her in any way, of course, but all of which assuaged the guilt of the gift-givers who mostly promptly forgot her and her daily horrific struggle through life.

Modern attention spans for the chronically ill are horribly short, probably because chronic or terminal illness in today's society is horribly tedious. Tedious, because we are all so uncomfortable with it.

Instead, too often, it is up to the sick and the dying to comfort the well and the un-dying.

Just take a moment to think about this, take a moment to see if you have ever experienced it yourself. The dying—sweet, stoic, silent—comforting those who are to be left behind. I know I experienced it when first I was diagnosed with cancer. I found myself in the completely unreal situation of having, over and over, to comfort people when I told them I had cancer. In the end I just stopped telling people, because almost invariably I was placed into the bizarre situation of comforting the well by saying everything would be all right (which, of course, it won't, but that's what people needed to hear to make them comfortable about me again).

The dying have been indoctrinated from a very young age into this sweet, stoic and silent state. They earn praise for always being "positive" and "bright" and "never complaining". Perhaps they are bright and positive and uncomplaining, but I am certain they lay in their beds with their fear and anger and grief and pain and frustration completely repressed while modern expectation forces them, the dying, to comfort the living.

I am sick of this tawdry game. I am sick to death of comforting people when all I want is to be comforted. I am sick of being abandoned by people for months on end only to be told eventually that "I knew they were thinking of me, right?" I am sick of being exhorted to be silent and sweet and stoic. I know I face a long and lonely death and no, I don't think I should just accept that.

I don't think I should keep *silent* about it.

I have witnessed many people die. As a child I watched my mother die a terrible death from the same cancer that is going to kill me. As a registered nurse for seventeen years I have seen scores of people die. I have watched the dying keep cheerful and reassuring while their family were there (forced by modern expectation of how people should die), only to break down and scream their terror when the family have gone. The one thing they all said, desperately, was "Don't let me die alone." But mostly they did die alone, doors closed on them by staff who were too frantically busy to sit with them, and relatives who have gone home and not thought to sit with their parent or sibling. People do die alone, and often not even with the slight comfort of a stranger nurse holding their hand. If you put your relative into a hospital or a hospice or a nursing home, then their chances of dying alone and uncomforted increase tremendously. I want to die at home, but I am realistic enough to know that my chances of that are almost nil as impersonal "carers" force me into a system that will remove me from any comfort I might have gained by dying in familiar, loved and comforting surroundings.

My mother, who died of the same cancer which will kill me, kept mostly stoic through three years of tremendous suffering. But I do remember one time, close to her death, when my father and I went to visit her in hospital. She was close to breaking point that evening. She wept, she complained, she expressed her fears in vivid, terrifying words. I recall how uncomfortable I was, and how relieved I was when she dried her tears and once more became cheerful and comforting herself. I was twelve at the time, and maybe I should feel no guilt about it, but I do now, for I know all too well how she felt, and how much she needed comforting far more than me.

She died in her cold impersonal hospital room in the early hours of the morning, likely not even with the comfort of a stranger nurse with her, certainly with none of her family there.

The great irony is that now I face the same death, from the same cancer.

That is the death that awaits many of us, me likely a little sooner than you, but in the great scheme of things that's neither here nor there. Not everyone dies alone, but many do.

Not everyone suffers alone, but most do it to some extent.

It is the way we have set up the modern art of death.

I am tired of the discomfort that surrounds the chronically and terminally ill. I am tired of the abandonment. I am tired of having to lie to people about how I am feeling just so I keep them around. I am tired of having to feel a failure when I need to confess to the doctor or nurse that the pain is too great and I need something stronger.

I am tired of being made to feel guilty when I want to express my fear and anguish and grief.

I am tired of keeping silent.

Sara Douglass
Nonsuch, 22 May 2010

ACKNOWLEDGEMENTS

"Of Fingers and Foreskins" copyright © 1995 Sara Douglass
Enterprises. First published in *Eidolon 21*, Penguin 1997.

"The Tower Room" copyright © 2011 Sara Douglass Enterprises.

"The Field of Thorns" copyright © 2000 Sara Douglass Enterprises.
First published in *Australian Women's Weekly*, October 2000.

"This Way to the Exit" copyright © 2008 Sara Douglass Enterprises.
First published in *Dreaming Again*, HarperCollins 2008.

"Fire Night" copyright © 2011 Sara Douglass Enterprises. First
published at saradouglass.com.

"The Rise of the Seneschal" copyright © 2011 Sara Douglass
Enterprises. First published at saradouglass.com.

"The Wars of the Axe" copyright © 2011 Sara Douglass Enterprises.
First published at saradouglass.com.

"How Axis Found His Axe" copyright © 2011 Sara Douglass
Enterprises. First published at saradouglass.com.

"How the Icarii Found Their Wings" copyright © 2011 Sara
Douglass Enterprises. First published at saradouglass.com.

"The Coroleans" copyright © 2011 Sara Douglass Enterprises. First
published at saradouglass.com.

"The Mistress of Marwood Hagg" copyright © 2003 Sara Douglass
Enterprises. First published in *Gathering The Bones*, 2003.

"Black Heart" copyright © 2011 Sara Douglass Enterprises. Appears
here for the very first time.

"St Uncumber" copyright © 1998 Sara Douglass Enterprises. First
published in *Australian Women's Weekly*, June 2001.

"The Evil Within" copyright © 1998 Sara Douglass Enterprises. First
published in *Dreaming Down Under*, 1998.

"Hall of Lost Footsteps" copyright © 2011 Sara Douglass Enterprises
and Angela Slatter. Appears here for the very first time.

"The Silence of the Dying" copyright © 2010 Sara
Douglass Enterprises. First published 22 May 2010 at
nonsuchkitchengardens.com. Appears here in print for the very
first time with the kind permission of Sara Douglass.

THANK YOU

The publisher would sincerely like to thank

Elizabeth Grzyb, Sara Douglass, Karen Brooks, Angela
Slatter, Jeremy G. Byrne, Juliet Marillier, Kim Wilkins, Isobel
Carmody, Kate Forsyth, Stephanie Smith, Jonathan Strahan,
Peter McNamara, Ellen Datlow, Grant Stone, Sean Williams,
Simon Brown, Garth Nix, David Cake, Simon Oxwell,
Grant Watson, Sue Manning, Steven Utley, Lisa L Hannett,
Bill Congreve, Jack Dann, Janeen Webb, Lucy Sussex, Stephen
Dedman, the Mt Lawley Mafia, the Nedlands Yakuza,
Amanda Pillar, Shane Jiraiya Cummings, Angela Challis,
Donna Maree Hanson, Kate Williams, Kathryn Linge,
Andrew Williams, Al Chan, Alisa and Tehani, Mel & Phil,
Hayley Lane, Georgina Walpole, everyone we've missed . . .

. . . and *you*.

IN MEMORY OF
Sara Warneke (1957–2011)
Eve Johnson (1945–2011)